P9-CCQ-771

Want A New, Better, Fantastic Job?

How To Find Satisfying Work In This Topsy-Turvy World

Pam Gross
Peter Paskill

CareerMakers Press
Portland, Oregon

Gross, Pam.
    Want a new better fantastic job? : how to find
    satisfying work in a topsy-turvy world / Pam
    Gross & Peter Paskill. – 2nd ed.
        p. cm.
        Includes index.
        LCCN: 99-60431
        ISBN: 0-9630012-1-3

    1. Job hunting – Handbooks, manuals, etc.
    2. Career changes – Handbooks, manuals, etc.
    3. Vocational guidance – Handbooks, manuals,
        etc. I. Paskill, Peter. II. Title.

HF5382.7.G76 2000   650.14
                           QBI00-764

Cover Design by
Tim Dickey and Ethan Firpo

CareerMakers Press
8555 S.W. Apple Way #130
Portland, OR 97225

What would your life be like
if you loved your work?
Want to find out?
www.careermakers.com

This Book is Dedicated to.......You !

change, of any sort, requires courage

-mary anne radmacher-

OUR HEARTFELT THANKS TO. . .

Every one of our thousands of CareerMakers graduates for sharing their stories, helping us develop job/career transition me - thods that work, and referring their friends and family to Career - Makers.

Our Human Resource friends—for helping people in significant ways by sending them to CareerMakers during downsizings, mer - gers, buy-outs and Acts of God, and for inviting us to help with in-house career management issues.

Ron Gross and Jana Paskill, our spouses for their belief in, and support of, our mission.

Anne Hudson—for exceptional commitment and masterful teach-ing.

Jim and Sally Petersen and the congregation of Southminster Presbyterian Church in Beaverton, Oregon for our roots.

Mary Anne Radmacher Hershey for her beautiful words and writ-ings to inspire your reading.

INTRODUCTION

The job search/career transition methods outlined in this book come from the authors' years of experience in the career management field. In 1982 Pam Gross founded CareerMakers to teach transition skills to people. She was joined in 1983 by Peter Paskill. Their business partnership has allowed CareerMakers to flourish and help thousands of people get on the path to find work they enjoy.

CareerMakers has continuously evolved over the years. Because program graduates stay in touch with Pam and Peter, their feedback on what works and what doesn't has allowed CareerMakers to constantly test methods and adapt as needed. This book reflects that evolution and the experiences of graduates. These methods work. They have been proved time and again. And, they can work for you.

IS THIS BOOK FOR YOU?

It certainly is if you know that a job search or a career transition is more about "employability" than it is about "employment." Our guess is that you could get a job (become employed) today if you had to. Getting a job isn't the problem. What you want is work worth doing...work that is in sync with your basic values, that uses your best skills and that is connected with something that's of interest to you. In order to find work worth doing, you must participate in an integrated process of self-reflection, learn how to talk and write about yourself and build supportive networks. These are the skills of transition which greatly enhance your employability by allowing you to market yourself into any number of satisfying situa - tions, no matter what you are doing now or have done in the past. Therefore, while this book is extremely helpful for those having to make a job/career transition because of being laid off, terminated, entering or re-entering the workforce, it is also appropriate for those who currently have a good job or career because these me - thods can be used within your present company to enhance your immediate position or change departments. And, because things can change so rapidly in today's work world, this book can be your "employability insurance".

Think about insurance. The prudent person buys insurance and

Page 6

hopes to never have to use it. We save money for a rainy day, but always hope for sunshine. So, too, we should prepare ourselves for job/career transitions...just in case.

By looking at your skills, interests and passions and under - standing the elements of gracious networking, interviewing and resume preparation as presented in this book, you are buying "em - ployability" insurance. When change comes your way, you will be able to walk into your future with a minimum of anxiety and a lot of know-how and confidence.

Therefore, if you are in the middle of a job search or career tran- sition, you will find invaluable information that you can put to use today. You will be much more effective and possibly shave weeks or months off your transition time. If you are currently employed in a job or career that you enjoy, the methods between these pages will greatly enhance it, while at the same time insuring that your next move is the right one.

LEFT BRAIN-RIGHT BRAIN

Because of the ever-changing, fast-paced world in which we live, you may find yourself feeling uneasy about your future. How do you market yourself? What technology do you need to know? What degrees are most likely to lead to a good job? What do "they" want anyway? How do I compare to the rest of the field? How can I find work that I enjoy doing? Who am I?

This book addresses all of those issues within a context of job/career transition methods. It is holistic and integrated in its ap - proach to transition. Therefore, it recognizes the importance of both the analytical and the emotional in the transition process. For ex - ample, the analytical is evidenced in methods regarding net - working, resumes, and interviewing. The emotional is evidenced in assessment and giving you an opportunity to think about the life you're living from a spiritual aspect. Our experience tells us that to conduct the job search or career transition without the right-brain work—Who am I? Why am I here? What are my best talents? What do I want?—is to end up in work that is unsatisfying time and again.

We hope that you will do the right-brain work to build your foun- dation for the transition. Words like "Creator" present in the first chapter may cause you discomfort. This is just a way to get you thinking about yourself. In fact, we have borrowed directly from an exercise that we do regularly at CareerMakers to create awareness of our clients' uniqueness. It is our goal for each reader to take him/herself seriously and "own" their one-of-a-kind uniqueness. Most of us don't know what makes us special—different from everyone else. And, we never will until we take the time to reflect and do the "inside" work.

FIND A FRIEND

We have discovered, from our personal experience as well as from our graduates, that trying to conduct a job search or career transition alone is both foolish and depressing. With no one to provide support, common sense and objectivity (the ability to ask the right questions), you will end up isolated, questioning your value and wondering what you're doing wrong. This results in adding months to your transition time and accepting jobs you really don't want.

Recruit a friend (better yet, friends) to help. Perhaps you know someone who would like to effect his/her own change of jobs or careers, and you can become each other's support system. Work through exercises together. Share values and interests. Write and share stories. Evaluate Compass information. Share names of people with whom to begin the process. Schedule weekly check-ins to assess progress. Having someone "in it with you" insures that you will operate with much more efficiency and a lot less anxiety. Or, after you have read the book, contact us if you wish and dis - cuss the possibility of participating in a CareerMakers seminar or some email- or tele-coaching.

Please call Pam or Peter toll-free, at 1-888-244-1055, or contact us by email at careers@careermakers.com.
Website: www.careermakers.com.

THE TEN TRUTHS OF JOB/CAREER TRANSITION

The relationships we've developed by being in the trenches with our program graduates as they maneuver the uncertain terrain of transition allowed us to formulate our "Ten Truths." You will find them interspersed throughout the text to illustrate our thoughts and methods. We thought you might like to see them listed on one page.

1) Until you take yourself seriously and come to know your skills, values and interests—the essence of who you are—it is unlikely that you will find enjoyable and satisfying work.

2) Whatever you believe to be the truth about the job market probably isn't.

3) Most jobs that are available this minute are not advertised anywhere. These jobs constitute the "hidden job market."

4) The prime rule of the job search is: Open your mouth and talk to people anyone, anytime, anywhere.

5) There is a structured and directed manner of accessing the hidden job market, and most people don't know how to do it effectively.

6) People hire people they know and like—whether or not they have the exact experience, background or skills to do the job.

7) Tell me how you will make me money, save me money or save me time, and I will seriously consider you as a candidate for a position in my company—whether or not I have an opening.

8) You do not need a resume to do a job search.

9) What "they" want is not nearly as important as what you want.

10) A successful job search is 20% analytical (technique and strategy) and 80% emotional (how you feel about yourself and your ability to relate to the rest of the world.)

Table of Contents

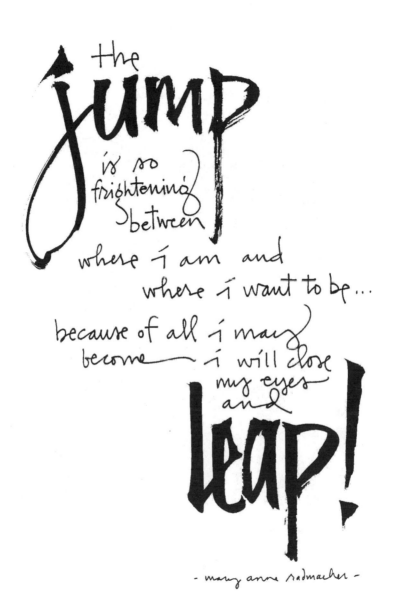

the
jump
is so
frightening
between
where i am and
where i want to be...
because of all i may
become — i will close
my eyes
and
leap!

- mary anne radmacher -

live with intention.
walk to the edge.
listen hard.

live

practice wellness.
laugh.
appreciate your friends.
play with abandon.
continue to learn.
choose with no regret

with
intention

do what you love.
live as if this is all there is.

— mary anne radmacher —

Chapter 1

How To Think About The Life You're Living

OLD LIFE
- What am I supposed to be doing with myself on this planet anyhow?
- I wish I had....
- Maybe next year...
- If only...
- Someday...

NEW LIFE
- How Can I use my Creator-given talents to make my best contribution to the world?
- How can I live a life of no regrets?
- What will I say in my Ulti - mate Interview?

THE REGRETFUL LIFE

What do you regret most in life. . .those things that you did but wish you hadn't, or those things you didn't do but wish you had? If you are like most Americans, you regret those things you didn't do but wish you had. According to a *Washington Post* survey, 61% of us are living a life fraught with regret.

Work without meaning can cause you to feel devalued, angry, depressed, and without hope. Being engaged in unsatisfying work, work which is out of sync with your skills, values, traits and in - terests, is a major contributor to living a life of regret. It can cause you to think, "If only things were different...," or, "Ten years ago I should have..." or, "Some day I'm going to..." Or, "I know there's something else out there for me." As one of our graduates said, "When I thought of what I might be/could be/should be doing with myself, I was filled with a profound wistfulness. It was so pervasive that I came to think of it as a chronic condition." Chronic wistful - ness is not the emotional state the Creator had in mind for human - kind, especially in a country that provides a myriad of oppor - tunities for its citizens to be all they want to be.

YOUR EMOTIONAL SIDE

Harold Kushner's book *When All You've Ever Wanted Isn't Enough* states that because of our fear of change "we choose a life of emotional flatness." Just imagine you have an emotional oscilloscope. You can plug it in and take a reading any time. What would the line on your print-out look like? Would it be a strong, rhythmic, flowing line with a broad range of regular highs and lows? If so, it would indicate a generally healthy enthusiasm for life with some wonderful peak experiences as well as some utterly miserable ones. Or, would the line on your oscilloscope be weak and erratic— mostly flat—with an occasional blip indicating a dash of excite - ment? ("Oh yes. I remember that blip. That was when I played tennis last July.")

Many of us are emotionally flatlined when it comes to our work. We are bored. We yearn for fulfillment. We yearn for excitement. We are beat down by what we do, yet we stay where we are. We fool ourselves by rationalizing that we really have no choice.

Because most of us do not willingly change jobs or careers, we choose to stay in emotionally flatlining work. One or several of the following could fit your circumstances:

*You might not like your job, but you stay because you are addicted to security. If you leave, you may not get your regular pay check fix with money, medical benefits and pension plan. The thought of withdrawal conjures visions of convulsions and hallucinations. So you choose the the real pain of staying over the imagined pain of leaving...forgetting that there is a transition period that will allow you to make excellent decisions as to whether you go or stay.

* You are fearful. The very thought of letting go of the security and comfort that you know—even if you hate it or are bored stiff by it—scares you to death.

* You might rationalize about yourself. You say things like, "Yes, but...it's not really so bad. My ulcers don't bother me too much, and I enjoy playing tennis on the weekends."

Your rationalizations extend to the job market. "There's nothing out there for me (at my age, without a degree, you fill in the blank _____).

Page 14

* You could be in denial of your self. You may never have taken the time to figure out what you're all about. Therefore, you are blind to your specialness. And so, you throw it away. You don't take yourself seriously as someone with unique traits, skills and values to contribute to the world.

* You don't know how to explore the myriad of possibilities which, in reality, exist for you in the world of work.

What is the result of choosing a life of emotional flatness and chronic wistfulness? Some day you will be looking back on your life. What do you want to say about your time on the planet?
"Well, I'm 80. I wish I had done things differently. I spent a lot of time doing things that weren't interesting to me or of much value to anyone else. If only..."

Or, "Well, I'm 80. By and large, I feel good about my life. I enjoyed my work and feel as though it was important to others, too. There's not much I would change if I could do it over again. I'm pleased with myself."

PERSPECTIVE

Let's get some perspective on your life...take stock of where you've been, where you are now and where you want to be in the future. Here's an exercise we do at CareerMakers. Look at the alphabet, on the following page, which is your life continuum. In order to get perspective, write the year you were born under the 0 at A. Then assume you are going to live to be 100 and write that year under the 100 at Z. In other words, if you were born in 1962, which is 0, you will be 100 in 2062.

Next, indicate where you are today on your life continuum. Do this by knowing that beginning with the letter B, each letter marks four years of your life. So, at B you were four years old, C eight, D twelve, and so on. The midpoint on the continuum has been marked at N or 52. You may count back from that midpoint, or forward, if that makes the task easier for you. When you have located the letter for your age (and it might fall in between two letters), write your current age under that letter. Finally, write this year under your age. Above the continuum, indicate where you are now by writing "I am here!" with an arrow pointing to your spot on the alphabet.

You should have three sets of dates and ages noted: when you were born which is 0 or A, when you will be 100 which is Z and where you are now.

YOUR LIFE CONTINUUM

A B C D E F G H I J K L M N O P Q R S T U V W X Y Z
0   52   100

INTROSPECTIVE

Now take a minute to ponder and write answers to these ques-tions:

How do you feel when you see where you are now on your life continuum?

How do you feel when you look back on your life from the pre-sent to 0? What are your regrets? You might want to note them. Then say, "Oh well. That's that. Time to move on."

Most important, what were your most gratifying times? Those times when you were engaged in life and feeling good about yourself? Having fun? Anticipating the days and weeks ahead?

GO FORTH!

No doubt you have heard from the pulpits of your churches or temples, "Go forth and use your Creator-given talents to make this planet a better place!" Or, perhaps you have become familiar with this philosophy through your reading of theology, metaphysics or self-help books. The underlying assumption is that the Creator has blessed you with specific gifts (skills, values, traits, interests) to contribute to the greater good. There is a cause-and-effect dynamic inherent in this thinking:

When you contribute your specific gifts you feel:

*Alive!	*Filled with Anticipation
*Energized	*Filled with Gratitude
*Engaged	*Peaceful Inside
*Enthusiastic	

As a result, you can't help but make the world a better place. Think about it this way: when you bestow your specific gifts upon creation, you are at a Checkpoint in your life, using those gifts to

Page 16

carry out the mission that your Creator wants you to fulfill. You feel alive, energetic and enthusiastic! Now, think about the times in your life that you have experienced a Checkpoint.

Checkpoints: Indicate your most gratifying times by placing a check under the appropriate letter on your life continuum and write a short description of what caused you to feel engaged, energized, enthusiastic and filled with anticipation. For example, ice skating beginning when I was six years old. Put a check between B and C. Under the check write "ice skating." Or, working on cars beginning when I was seventeen. Put a check between E and F. Or, teaching school when I was twenty-four. Put a check under G and write "teaching." Or, when I was at home taking care of my kids at 32. Or, coaching Little League at 38. Or, the project I spearheaded last year at work when I was 42. Or, being in charge of my church's building committee when I was 51. **Mark as many Checkpoints as you can on your Continuum.**

BEYOND Z...THE ULTIMATE INTERVIEW

Let's suppose that after Z on your life continuum you will have a conversation with the Creator. This conversation will be about your life. The Creator will gently ask you to speak of how you used your gifts for the betterment of humankind. How will you respond? "I regret that I didn't use my gifts better," or, "When I was thirty-four (or forty-five, or fifty-three, or sixty-six) on my life continuum, I got it! From then on, **I made the conscious decision to create Checkpoints in my life.**" Ask yourself what you want your conversation—we call it the Ultimate Interview—to be about. What, in this final interview, are you going to impart about the contributions you have made?

ELLEN

Ellen was working in a job she did not like, with people she was not happy to be around. She did not look forward to going to work, and she did not know what her life work should be about. Through the CareerMakers process, she began to get a glimpse of what meaningful work would be for her. Her assignment was to write her "Beyond Z" conversation. As you continue to make your way through this book, you will see that Ellen has made use of the interviewing methods in Chapter 5 and the assessment format in

Chapter 2 in her ultimate interview with the Creator. Since it can be said that our methods prepare you for that final interview, it is safe to say that this book is also about mortality management.

ELLEN'S ULTIMATE INTERVIEW:

Ellen: Hello, Creator. It's a pleasure to meet with you again.

Creator: Sit down, Ellen. I've been looking forward to talking with you. How did you like your visit on Earth?

Ellen: Well I never thought I would make it 100 years. I loved the time I spent there! I met thousands of people, and I enjoyed ex - ploring the wonderful oceans and mountains. Most of all, though, I enjoyed attaining my goal for being there in the first place.

Creator: Well, you had a lot of work to do, and I wanted to make sure you had enough time to fulfill your obligations. Now, I know you would like to enter the pearly gates, but can you explain to me why I should let you in?

Ellen: I believe I've earned entrance because I have accomplished what you intended me to accomplish. I know I was supposed to leave the world a better place than when I arrived, and I've done that.

Creator: Oh, really. Can you give me some examples?

Ellen: Well, I got on track when I was at H on my life continuum, or 34. Before that I was lost in the abyss, depressed and full of "If onlies" and "I wish I hads". But, when I started writing some of my life Skill Stories, it became evident that you equipped me with unique gifts to help me accomplish specific goals.

The most important skills you gave me were **interpersonal communications, motivating others,** and **writing.** The most impor - tant traits you bestowed upon me were being **proactive, genuine** and **purposeful.** And then the things I was most enthusiastic about were **children, the environment** and **teaching**. After I figured all of this out, I began the New Way search to find a way to put all of these elements to good use...to intentionally create Checkpoints for myself and to please you as well. For example, I initiated and de - veloped an environmental camp for inner city children.

Creator: That's wonderful, Ellen! How did you do that?

Ellen: When I was a child, I loved going to my Great Aunt Nellie's house in the country. So, I envisioned converting a run-down ranch into an environmental camp for children who would not ordinarily have an opportunity to commune with nature. I purchased an abandoned ranch with little cottages on it located in a spectacular wooded area near snowcapped mountains and alpine lakes. I rehabilitated the ranch and called it "Aunt Nellie's Wonder ranch."

I taught children about wildlife and the sensitivity of their na - tural habitats. I counseled kids in need using my interpersonal communication skills. I instilled environmental values into thousands of children using my motivation skills.

I persuaded parents, industries and legislators to fund the camp using my writing skills. I promoted my passion for environmental awareness by using my traits of being genuine and purposeful.

The results of my efforts were: The camp is still going strong 40 years after I started it. I received enthusiastic feedback from my former campers indicating I had made a significant contribution to their lives. I enjoyed getting up every morning. I accomplished my mission to make the world a better place.

Creator: That is a very impressive story, Ellen. Another example?

Ellen: Let me tell you about how, after I retired from Aunt Nellie's Wonder ranch, I used that experience and my writing skills to pen my autobiography called *The Hard Way to a Simple Life.*

I collected and analyzed data, tabulating the differences in my life before and after H on my life continuum. In my book I stressed the importance of taking stock of your life and to stop putting limita - tions on yourself. I provided many examples of how I became happy first and then successful. I expressed gratitude for the many people who were part of my life. I created a legacy that can be handed down to future generations.

Creator: *And the results were*?

Ellen: My autobiography was on the NY Times bestseller list for 15 weeks. My book inspired others to lead a positive and fulfilling life like mine. The proceeds from the book went to others who wanted to start their own environmental camp. I had fun writing it. Do these examples illustrate the fulfillment of my mission?

Creator: Indeed! It seems as though you made excellent use of your gifts.

Ellen: Once I began creating Checkpoints, I used my gifts to do your work. I'm proud of my accomplishments. I feel that I have honed my skills so well on Earth that I know I can work miracles behind the pearly gates.

Creator: Ellen, thank you for all your hard work and for spending this time with me today. I will review your file and let you know my decision next week.

Ellen: It was a privilege to serve you. And, if I haven't heard from you by Tuesday afternoon, may I call to check on my status?

Creator: Yes, you may. Honestly, people like you who actually **DO** that stuff that Pam and Peter talk about--completing the Compass, BRIDGING, finding Checkpoints-- can be a real pain in the rump sometimes. On the other hand, you inspire me because you exemplify exactly what I had in mind when I invented human beings in the first place!

CONSCIOUS CAREERING: DO THE WORK

Is Ellen working with kids on her ranch? Not yet. But, she's doing the research to see how to recombine her skills and interests to do something meaningful with kids and the environment. For her that's work worth doing.

Wherever you are on your life continuum, and no matter what your work and life have been in the past, you have the ability to build a new future by consciously creating Checkpoints in your life. Your next step is to **do the work** of self-assessment, because doing the work means you are taking yourself seriously.

vital life

a key to a vital life is an eagerness to learn and a willingness to change.

- maryanne radmacher -

craft your vision.
establish
your standard.

celebrate

excellence.

determine
your measure.

exceed your own expectations.
ask for what you want.

- mary anne radmacher -

Chapter 2

How To Find Direction: Your Compass

OLD WAY
What Counts:
- Past job experience
- Past job titles
- Degrees
- Diplomas
- Certificates
- Tests/Evaluations

NEW WAY
What Counts:
- A sense of purpose
- Compass ...
- Interests/Passions
- Transferable Skills, Values and Traits
- Relationships

Job Search Truth #1

Until you take yourself seriously and come to grips with your skills, values, traits and interests...the essence of who you are...you are not likely to find enjoyable and satisfying work.

OLD WAY ASSESSMENT

The Old Way search is predicated upon your specific past ex - perience, job titles, degrees, diplomas and certificates. Old way thinkers believe they fill in the missing pieces of themselves by tak- ing tests—MMPI, Meyers/Briggs, etc. While these tests and eval - uations may provide you with information about yourself, you end up with more "bits and pieces" rather than an integrated and holistic picture of yourself and what you want in your work. Without any new understanding of skills, values, traits and interests, you are likely to stick with what is familiar...what you've always done, even though you know in your heart that there are other exciting things out there for you to do.

NEW WAY ASSESSMENT

The New Way search is predicated upon all that you already know about yourself—and more. New Way thinkers know that their transferable skills will carry them into new career fields. They understand that they have many options available to them in addition to what they have done in the past. Career changers have recombined their skills, values and traits in new ways and marketed them into exciting new career arenas. Others found work they enjoy in their current industries. These people see themselves as dynamic and having much to offer, rather than feeling stuck in a box defined by their past work experiences.

Tough Reality: Self-assessment is the work nobody wants to do. Yet, it is critical to finding satisfying work. And, all the exercises, computer print-outs, counseling and group work in the world will not give you what you crave: THE ANSWER. You want to know now and absolutely what your next job or career should/will be. You want to know the job title. You believe you must know this before you can start your search.

It is not the purpose of assessing skills, values, traits and interests to give you this answer. It is the purpose of self-assessment to give you clues, ideas and information on the things (plural) that you **might** want to do in the future.

Tougher Reality: It is these clues, ideas and information that form the foundation of your job/career transition. The answers (plural) about possibilities for your future come from the Researching process.

YOUR COMPASS
This chapter makes you wrestle with a series of exercises that culminates in putting vital information on your Compass. When it is complete, your Compass will provide you with a tangible picture of what you need to be happy on the job. Thus, your job/career transition becomes a quest to find what fits your Compass. Your Compass gives you focus and direction. It is best to do your Compass work in a notebook, writing in pencil. Cross out, erase, slash and rip until you get your Compass to reflect what you want!

ASSESSING #1: INTEREST IDENTIFICATION
It seems that the only job/career transition worth doing is one that is interest-driven. If you stick with your interests (take them seriously), your search for enjoyable work can be a lot of fun. Yes...fun!

Page 24

It seems that the longer we are on this planet, the more separated we become from our true selves. We forget things about our lives that were important to us. We sublimate our interests to others: spouses, significant others, partners, parents, kids. We work at jobs that pay the bills, but to which we have little emotional attachment. We feel 'ho-hum' about our work rather than excited about the daily, weekly challenges.

Those reasons, and others that you may think of, make the case for digging around in your past to see what interests are buried there. One word we think should appear in Webster's Dictionary is "yoosta." As in, "I yoosta ski." "I yoosta create fascinating envir - onments for tropical fish." "I yoosta love to work on cars." "I yoosta do a lot of knitting and sewing." "I yoosta invent things." What did **you** yoosta do that you enjoyed?

SNAPSHOTS

The purpose of Snapshots is to help you reflect upon your past and become reacquainted with yourself. This exercise is ongoing in nature. You cannot just sit down for an hour and complete it. In fact, it is not really possible to complete it simply because you cannot remember everything about your past. However, the more informa - tion you can excavate, the better you will know yourself.

THREE CONCRETE VALUES IN DOING THIS EXERCISE

1. You will find clues as to the things that pique your enthusiasm, interest. Since interests provide the base of any job/career transition, Snapshots could give you ideas on where to begin.

2. You will get in touch with past successes. You need to do this in order to write Skill Stories. Much information for your stories can come from Snapshots.

3. You will be a better interviewing candidate. Since articulating skills in job interviews means using illustrations from your past, Snapshots also provides a base for job interview preparation. This is especially valuable when you find yourself in "behavioral" or "competency-based" interviews, and write skills-aligned resumes as illustrated in Chapters 4 and 5.

YOUR LIFE IN PICTURES

You know all those snapshots you have of family gatherings, events and vacations? Well, find them. If you are a left brainer, they will be found in neat albums. If you are a right brainer, you will gather them up from various drawers and cubby holes. Your snap - shots are reminders of your past. Thumb through them and record pertinent information using the following formats. Let the pictures trigger other events and record them as well.

CHILDHOOD SNAPSHOTS
Ages 0 - 12

Significant people in my life:
Call one or two and ask what you were like from ages 0 - 6 before you got caught up in the "system" of school where you had to color within the lines, line up for lunch and raise your hand to speak.

My favorite toys/games/pets? My favorite school subjects activities?
Things I learned about: (For example: soccer, birds, tropical fish)
Highlights of my childhood years:

ADOLESCENT SNAPSHOTS
Ages 13 - 18
Significant people:
Favorite school subjects/activities:
Jobs:
Things I learned about:
Highlights of my adolescence and lessons learned:

YOUNG ADULT SNAPSHOTS
Ages 19 - 32
Significant people:
Jobs:
Companies/Titles
Volunteer work:
Things I learned about:
Fun/leisure/hobbies:
Highlights and lessons learned:

ADULT SNAPSHOTS
Ages 33 - 45
Significant people:
Jobs:
Companies/Titles
Volunteer work:
Things I learned about:
Fun/leisure/hobbies:
Highlights and lessons learned:

MIDDLE ADULT SNAPSHOTS I
Ages 46 - 56
Significant people:
Jobs:
Companies/Titles
Volunteer work:
Things I learned about:
Fun/Leisure/Hobbies:
Highlights and lessons learned:

MIDDLE ADULT SNAPSHOTS II
Ages 57 - 67
Significant people:
Jobs:
Companies/Titles
Volunteer work:
Things I learned about:
Fun/Leisure/Hobbies:
Highlights and lessons learned:

REFLECTING
What, if any, threads of interests do you see running through your Snapshots? What had you forgotten about that this exercise brought back to you? Sometimes what's missing is as important as what was included. What's missing that you would like to bring into your life? What conclusions can you draw from "Lessons Learned?" What insights, clues did you gain from these Snapshots?

Write a statement telling how you feel about your life as you have lived it so far.

MORE INTERESTS

Here are some direct questions to answer to discover interests:

1) What "stuff" do you like? Look around your house, garage and basement. What things do you enjoy. "I love my radial arm saw!" exclaimed one fellow. There's a clue.

2) What issues and causes are you curious and/or passionate about? Drunk driving? Feminism? Specific health issues? Save the Whales?

3) What industries, companies or job titles do you wonder about?

4) What would you do with yourself if you won the lottery? After you had indulged yourself and the thrill was gone, what would you do with your life? You could do anything you wanted and be a smashing success...what would that be?

5) Spiritually speaking, how would you use your Creator-given talents to make this planet/nation/society/state/city better than it is now?

DISTILLING: I WONDER...?

As you think about your interests, think in terms of which ones you would like to know more about. Key words in interest selection are, "I wonder...?" If tennis is one of your interests, you could be thinking, "I wonder how I might fit into the tennis industry." Or, "I wonder what Acme Widget, Inc. is like as a company to work for." Or, "I wonder what a mechanical engineer really does." Select no more than five interests that you would like to explore. These can be industries, companies, job titles or going into business for yourself. Try to be as specific as possible, avoiding things such as 'working with people' or 'reading' or 'marketing.' Ask yourself, "Marketing what?" The answer will give you a concrete interest to pursue.

Using a pencil (in case you want to make changes later), write your interest selections in the middle of your Compass. It is alright to add and subtract interests as you reflect and learn more about what genuinely interests you.

ASSESSING #2: VALUES

The People Profile, Work Values, Life Values, Working Conditions, Location and Money exercises will cause you to think and evaluate. Each of these six exercises will culminate with writing your top five values in the appropriate segment of your Compass. Realize that this is not a marathon...no one is running at your heels. Take time to be thoughtful. Take time to examine yourself and your wants. Take time to talk with others about the outcomes of your exercises. Take time to deliberate and reflect. Take time.

PEOPLE PROFILE

If you could surround yourself with ideal people in an ideal work environment, check the ten traits that those people would exhibit:

☐Good communicators

☐Easy-going

☐Fair-minded

☐Goal-oriented

☐Able to say they made a mistake(Humble—not ego-driven)

☐Optimistic

☐Of high integrity

☐Direct (I know where I stand)

☐Visionary

☐Competitive

☐Authentic (Is him/herself consistently)

☐Professional

☐Trusting

☐Competent

☐Risk-takers

☐Appreciative of humor

☐Democratic

☐Honest

☐Considerate of my personal wants/needs

☐Good listeners

☐Accepting of all kinds of people

☐Good delegators

Add any traits that are important to you that do not appear on our list.

Thoughtfully hone your list to the five traits that must be present in the people with whom you work and write them on your Compass in the People segment.

WORK VALUES

Check the ten work values that you feel you must have on the job to be happy and productive. You function best in an environment that offers you:

- ☐ Independence
- ☐ Open communication
- ☐ Advancement
- ☐ The ability to make decisions
- ☐ Great responsibility
- ☐ Moderate responsibility
- ☐ Little responsibility
- ☐ A fast work pace
- ☐ Moderate work pace
- ☐ Security (long-term employment)
- ☐ Physical challenge
- ☐ Stimulating co-workers
- ☐ Learning opportunities
- ☐ Humor in the workplace
- ☐ Time freedom
- ☐ Flexibility
- ☐ Moral/spiritual fulfillment
- ☐ Power and authority
- ☐ The sharing of ideas
- ☐ Creativity
- ☐ A team approach
- ☐ Moderate structure
- ☐ Lots of structure
- ☐ Diversity

Add any work values that are important to you but do not appear on our list.

Thoughtfully hone your list to the five work values that must be present in your workplace and write them in the Work Values segment of your Compass.

LIFE VALUES

Check the ten Life Values that are most important to you. If you do not like our definition of a value, write your own.

Achievement — strong desire to accomplishment impressive things

Meaningful Work — do work that truly matters to me...and earn money

Adventure — seek much exploration, risk, excitement

Authenticity — able to be myself (the same self) at home, with friends, at work

Personal Freedom — want independence, to make my own choices, be in control

Expertness — be good at something important to me

Service — want to contribute to other's lives

Leadership — have influence and authority

Money — aspire to have plenty of money for the things I want

Spirituality — find meaning for my life, develop set of core beliefs

Physical health — strive to be fit, live healthy lifestyle

Emotional health — develop the ability to handle inner conflict competently

Work — find a job to make enough to take care of my basic needs

Affection — build close, warm, caring relationships

Wisdom — have mature understanding, insights

Family — create good relationships and contented living situation

Recognition — be well-known, have prestige

Pleasure — have fun, satisfaction, enjoyment

Security — be financially sound with a stable future

Self-growth — pursue on-going personal development and exploration

Add any life values that are important to you but do not appear on our list.

Thoughtfully hone your list to the five life values that should define and govern the basic life/work choices you make.

WORKING CONDITIONS

Check the things that are most important to you in your work environment. Distill your checks to the five conditions you <u>must have</u> to feel good and perform well.

On-the-job activity level:
0-------------------100
(morgue)   (New York Stock Exchange)

Area:
city center
urban neighborhood
suburban
rural

Company Size:
small (2-50 people)
medium (50 - 200 people)
large (201 - 800 people)
corporate (801 - thousands)

Physical setting:
accessible by public transportation
free parking
luxurious facility
simple surroundings
green spaces
walk to shops, restaurants
air conditioning
safety (worker programs, neighborhood)
state of the art equipment and tools
natural light, windows
telecommuting possible

Work space:
private office
modular space
open floor

Dress code:
professional (suits, dresses)
casual (slacks, skirts, sweaters)
laid back (jeans, tee-shirts, pajamas)
flexible depending upon work activity on any given day

Amenities:
employee lounge
cafeteria
smoking area
health/fitness facility

Working hours:
day
swing
graveyard
split

Compensation:
straight commission
base plus commission
exempt (salaried)
non-exempt (hourly plus overtime)
Travel:
% car
% plane
% time away from home
Add any working conditions that are important to you but do not appear on our list. Select your five most important working conditions and write them in the appropriate segment of your Compass.

LOCATION
Which five of the following are you most important considerations in choosing where you live?

Population of_____
Lifestyle: urban/suburban/rural
Climate_____
Commute to work: miles/time_____
Geographical topography_____
Cost of living
Feeling of safety
Strong educational system (schools, libraries, colleges)
Good medical facilities

Good transit system: easy access to trains, airports, decent streets, public transportation
Environmentally clean
Friendly, neighborly people
Near family/friends
Cultural opportunities (theaters, concerts, movies, lectures, seminars, etc.)
Close-knit community
Professional sports teams
Cultural diversity
Dynamic political scene
Recreational opportunities: lakes, oceans, mountains, rivers
Good city planning/government
Good restaurants

Add your own items that make a place livable for you.
Write the five most important things you need in a geographical area and then write them in the appropriate segment of your Compass.

MONEY

It is helpful to take a realistic look at the money you want to make. To do this, start with what you are making now. Do some budgeting to arrive at SURVIVAL, BASIC NEEDS+ and IDEAL.

Present
Including all sources of income, state your current annual earnings:
$_____

Survival
If you found a smashing job --one that you would love to show up to each day, what minimum salary would you accept in order to take the job, assuming more money would be forthcoming?
$_____

Basic needs +
Considering your present needs, what salary would cause you to feel comfortable: all bills paid, including savings and things like college funds plus some left for fun/recreation?
$_____

Ideal
Looking at the ideal, how much would you like to make? Based on your current skills, education and experience, what do you feel you

could realistically expect — top dollar? $_____

List benefits you feel you absolutely need:

> Medical
> Dental
> Vision
> Retirement/Pension
> Stock Options
> Profit Sharing
> Paid Vacation/Sick Leave
> Child Care
> Elder Care
> Disability
> Tuition Reimbursements
> Sabbaticals

Write figures for each category—Present, Survival, Basic+ and Ideal in the appropriate segment of your Compass.

ASSESSING #3: SKILLS AND TRAITS

Many companies are focusing heavily on hiring employees who "fit" the company culture. Therefore, you must know your traits and skills, and how to articulate them, so that you can research and target companies that will "fit" you. That way you are not only hired for what you can do for a company (your skills), but for who you are (your traits). And, it's a win-win hiring experience.

The following pages contain skill sets, skill words and traits. Fundamentally, a skill is defined as something you can do... "I can," and a trait is a descriptor... "I am." Take time to familiarize yourself with these pages. Pick up that pencil and check the skills that you have **enjoyed** using on the job, at home or in a volunteer capacity. Since these lists are limited, please add skills and traits that you know you have but are not found on the lists.

SKILL SETS

Skill Set: Sales/Marketing
selling
presenting
influencing
meeting quotas

promoting
prospecting
negotiating
motivating

Skill Set: Project Management
communicating
delegating
decision-making
directing
goal-setting
motivating
listening
budgeting

Skill Set: Manual/Mechanical
assembling
building
installing
maintaining equipment
operating machinery
repairing
fixing/remodeling

Skill Set: Analytical/Technical
reasoning
evaluating
monitoring
systematizing
analyzing data
troubleshooting
investigating
gathering information

Skill Set: Training/Teaching
developing programs
speaking
facilitating
listening
writing

assessing needs
developing rapport
motivating

Skill Set: Communication
interviewing
teaching
counseling
writing/editing
summarizing
presenting
interpreting

Skill Set: Creativity
starting new things
envisioning
inventing
writing
innovating
designing
thinking with both sides
of your brain
painting/drawing/weaving/
sculpting/etc.

Skill Set: Computer
word processing
spread sheets
graphics
CD Rom
Internet
designing Web pages
building computers
programming
networking

Skill Set: Interpersonal
advising
counseling
consulting

listening
mediating
giving feedback
maintaining:
objectivity
tact/diplomacy
confidentiality

Skill Set: Administration
juggling many activities
meeting deadlines
processing information
listening
working under pressure
following instructions
relating well
technical skills:
keyboarding
word processing
calculator
email
phone systems
copiers/faxes

Write any skill set that you possess but is not illustrated here:

SKILLS WORDS
"I can..."

accomplish
achieve
activate
adapt
adjust
administer
advise
allocate
analyze
approve
arbitrate
arrange
ascertain
assemble
assess
assign
assimilate
assist
assure
attain
bring about
budget
build
calculate
clarify
classify
clean
coach
collect
command
commend
communicate
compare
compile
complete
compose
compute
conceptualize

conduct
consolidate
construct
consult
contact
contribute
control
cooperate
coordinate
correlate
counsel
create
cultivate
dance
decide
define
delegate
deliver
demonstrate
design
determine
develop
diagnose
direct
discover
dispense
display
dissect
distribute
document
draft
dramatize
draw
edit
employ
encourage
enforce
engineer
enhance
envision

equip
establish
evaluate
examine
execute
expand
expedite
experiment
explain
extract
facilitate
fashion
file
fix
follow up
follow orders
forecast
formulate
gather
generate
guide
handle
head
hire
identify
illustrate
imagine
improve
improvise
increase
influence
inform
initiate
innovate
inspect
inspire
install
instigate
instill
institute

instruct
integrate
interface
interpret
interview
introduce
invent
investigate
juggle many activities
keyboard
kindle
launch
lecture
lead
listen
maintain
market
master
mediate
meet quotas
monitor
motivate
negotiate
nominate
obtain
operate
optimize
orchestrate
originate
oversee
paint
participate
perceive
perfect
perform
persuade
pilot
pioneer
play
predict

prepare
prescribe
present
prioritize
problem-solve
process
produce
program
project
promote
propose
prove
provide
publish
purchase
qualify
quantify
question
ramrod
reason
receive
recognize
recommend
reconcile
record
recruit
rectify
reevaluate
refer
refine
regulate
rehabilitate
relate
remodel
reorganize
repair
report
represent
research
retrieve

revamp
review
revise
revitalize
revive
schedule
select
sell
set goals
shape
simplify
solve
spearhead
stimulate
structure
supervise
teach
test
train
translate
troubleshoot
upgrade
utilize
win
work under pressure
write

Add some of your own:

TRAITS
"I am..."

accepting
active
altruistic
ambitious
angry
articulate
assertive
authentic
bold
brazen
bright
calculating
calm
caring
charismatic
clever
collaborative
committed
compassionate
competitive
comprehensive
confident
conscientious
controlled
courageous
creative
curious
detailed
diligent
diplomatic
disciplined
domestic
dynamic
easy-going
economical
efficient
empowering

energetic
engaging
enterprising
enthusiastic
even-tempered
flamboyant
flexible
focused
forthright
frugal
fun-loving
genuine
goal-oriented
gutsy
handy
hardworking
healthy
holistic
honest
humorous
imaginative
impulsive
independent
industrious
influential
insightful
intelligent
introspective
invested
involved
kind
lively
loving
methodical
multi-faceted
natural
nurturing
open
optimistic
outgoing

patient
peaceful
personable
persuasive
physical
positive
powerful
practical
principled
proactive
reliable
reserved
resilient
resourceful
responsive
results-oriented
self-assured
sensitive
sentimental
serious
sincere
spunky
strong
stubborn
supportive
sweet
talented
technical
thorough
thoughtful
tough-minded
trouble-shooter
unafraid
understanding
versatile
visionary
zealous

Your Additions:

STORIES THAT ILLUSTRATE YOUR SKILLS

Now, supposing that you checked the skill of facilitating. You might think, "I remember working awfully hard to get those doctors into a new clinic: a thousand details, deadlines, new information to process and a lot of pressure...and I enjoyed every minute of it!" Then write about that experience using the format *What. How.Wow!*

It looks like this:

Skill:
Facilitating

What I did.
I facilitated a major relocation for a team of doctors.

How I did it.
I directed the decision-making process.
I researched suitable locations.
I developed a detailed expense analysis and budget ($200,000)
I collaborated with the architect to design the space.
I researched custom vs modular cabinetry
I coordinated with the architect, contractor and building manager
   to stay within budget.
I supervised the move.

Note: Skill words are underlined.

Wow! (Results)
The doctors were delighted with their new space.
The doctors received a letter from the building manager that my close monitoring saved about $10,000.
I loved developing a plan and driving it through to completion.
I received a $2500 bonus.

Each skill word is underlined, indicating that you "can do" it. You can coordinate, facilitate, research, develop and collaborate. What isn't underlined, but implied, are the skills of budgeting, designing, decision-making and juggling many activities. Results paint the picture of you as someone who gets things done in an

Page 44

economical manner. This story infers that you are creative, re-sourceful, reliable and industrious...traits. Obviously you were a valued employee, as your efforts were handsomely rewarded.

As you can see, **a skill story provides a tangible, measurable example of your skills and traits.** Skill stories also provide insights into your interests and values. Therefore, the more stories you write, the more clear you become on your skills, traits, interests and values. And, stories provide your foundation for writing resumes and interviewing.

EXAMPLES THAT ILLUSTRATE YOUR TRAITS

It is very powerful to be able to give examples of your traits in interviews and on resumes because most people simply list them and hope they sound good. In fact, everyone claims the same traits. "I'm loyal, reliable, resourceful, creative, blah, blah, blah." Aren't you? Of course. Unless you come up with examples to illustrate traits, you will sound like everyone else. Write trait examples so that you can say things like, "I'm resourceful. For example, when I needed money to take a seminar, I held a garage sale and made enough for the tuition." Or, "I'm a team player. When my co-work-er needed time off to care for her sick child, I covered her work for her." Or, "I'm resilient. When I broke my ankle, I worked from home for a week and then got rides to the office where I worked about half time. After two weeks, I was contributing 100%."

These concrete examples leave a picture with the interviewer or the reader of your skills-aligned resume.

CHECKPOINTS AGAIN

If you enjoyed facilitating the relocation of the doctors, it is like-ly you also enjoyed directing other projects. Go back to Snapshots, add as much information as you can and highlight the things you did that were enjoyable, satisfying and fun for you..when you en - joyed the experience and were happy with the outcome. Given the experience and outcome, you might like to do something like it again -- not necessarily the exact thing, but something like it. There was something about doing that particular thing that made you feel good inside, and if you could do something like it again, you would feel good inside again. **It does not matter if this is job-related.** It only matters that, on balance, you would do it again if the opportun-ity arose.

For example, a Checkpoint for you might be planning family

vacations. You might have received great satisfaction from building your deck, or landscaping your yard. You might have had fun doing that special assignment at work. You might feel great about re-storing your old MG. You might feel proud of resolving a personnel conflict at work, or you loved the challenge of putting the company picnic together. **Your stories come from every single facet of your life, and each one tells much about you!** And, no matter which facet of your life they come from, they could be useful in interviews and on resumes. So, instead of being confined to one facet of your life for assessment: Work, including degrees, diplomas, certificates and past job titles, **your entire life is open to the process**. This assessment method helps to give you a clear picture of who you are and which skills and traits you want to use in the world of work. Hence, we call it "clarifying."

WRITE FIVE STORIES NOW!

Your immediate task is to write five stories using the What.How.Wow! format. Share your stories with a friend. Read them aloud and write the skills and traits that come from those stories. Get feedback from your friend on skills and traits. What did you learn about yourself from the story?

Given that you're going to use skills on a daily and weekly basis, what five skills would you enjoy using most on the job? Reflect upon the skills you have assessed from your stories and select the five skills that would make you wake up in the morning with a smile on your face, knowing you "get to" do speaking, analyzing and creating on that day. And that you can show up and be appreciated for your traits of being authentic, honest and supportive. Furthermore, you will be appreciated and rewarded for the contribution your skills and traits make to the organization or to your own business.

Put the five skills and traits in the appropriate segment of your Compass. Your Compass is complete!

YOUR STORY FILE: SEE APPENDIX D

In order for you to participate in an ongoing process of clarifying your skills, values, traits and interests, we suggest that you compile a personal story file. Using the format **What.How.Results (Wow!)** begin writing skill stories and trait examples and put them in a computer file or a manila folder. Your ultimate goal is to write upwards of 20 stories initially and then continue to add to your file as you think of or develop new stories. Use as a format the story on page 44 or Appendix D. Practice telling your stories out loud!

RESILIENT, RESPONSIVE, NIMBLE, DYNAMIC!!!!

These words describe how the New Way person operates in today's job market. Self-assessment is absolutely critical in attaining this level of functioning. Imagine that you have created a file of twenty or so stories each of which tells much about you. Imagine that you are asked for a resume or invited to an interview. Imagine opening your story file and selecting stories that will illustrate your skills as they relate to that specific opening. No more sitting in front of the blank screen (or paper) trying to dredge examples from the abyss of your mind—they are already com - pleted! Target your resume for a particular position, select stories that illustrate your skills and write your skills-aligned resume. And, when you have a job interview, prepare for it by practicing telling your stories out loud. We call this developing the skill of articu - lating.

Your story file provides you with a bedrock of confidence and allows you to perform extraordinarily when interviewing and writ - ing resumes. Indeed, doing this hard work means that you are, at last, taking yourself seriously as a unique human being with much to offer. Go!

JOE'S NEW JOB

One of our graduates wrote about how a networking opportunity led him to a position which was extremely challenging and fit his Compass...a product engineer. His note said:

I am convinced that my assessment at CareerMakers prepared me for the resulting interviewing and evaluation process.
Here's how:

1) Skill stories — truly an amazing process of introspection and enhancing my abilities to articulate what I have accomplished.

2) My Compass — a significant tool in realizing that this position fit most of the critical elements. The Compass clarified my thinking and helped me make a good decision.

3) Support — ny friends, family and you guys supported me in reaching out and grabbing this opportunity.

I will continue to use New Way skills on the job so as to take ad - vantage of new opportunities as my company expands.

Stop by the company, and I'll buy you a cup of coffee.

Joe

Your thoughts and notes:

the
challenge
which
stands
before
you
is to delight
in the
unknown and
dare the taste
of possibility.

- mary anne radmacher -

Chapter 3

HOW TO FIND OR CREATE SATISFYING WORK

OLD WAY

Based on past work life
- Write Resume
- Find openings:
  Want ads
  Company hotlines
  Headhunters/recruiters
  Employment agencies
  Internet
- Send a resume to openings
- Wait for response
- Attend interviews
- Receive offers...maybe
- Wonder, "Is this right for me?"
- Take job like one you left

NEW WAY

Based on Compass
- Extend yourself:
  Build relationships
  Research interests
  Busybody
- Generate job interviews:
  Write skills-aligned resume
  Prepare stories for job interview
- Weigh offers:
  Filter information through your Compass
  Make solid career decision
- Show up to work that is enjoyable and fulfilling

THE NEW WAY

The New Way job/career transition involves learning new ways of thinking and new ways of operating. That means you must unlearn old habits of thought and behavior. This isn't easy and can cause anxiety as you replace the old with the new.

The anxiety begins with the understanding that finding work the New Way is **not** about job titles. It is **not** about resumes. It is **not** about human resource departments. It is **not** about the Sunday want ads. It is **not** about hours spent in front of your PC on the Internet. It is **not** about the safety and comfort of your home. That's Old Way stuff.

The New Way job search **is** about you and what interests you. It **is** all about enthusiasm and excitement. It **is** about designing your job and naming it yourself. It **is** about human beings helping other human beings. It **is** about getting out of your house and researching your interests. It **is**, finally, about creating Checkpoints in your work-life: work that energizes your spirit and keeps you smiling.

A NETWORKING PROCESS: THE WORLD IS NOT FLAT

The New Way job search is a finely tuned, structured networking process that helps you make wise career decisions and end up doing work you enjoy. As it applies to the job search, networking requires a specific and sophisticated set of skills which **none of us has been taught** in junior high, senior high or college. The basic skill that needs to be learned is that of "extending" — putting your **self** into the world as an explorer to discover what's "out there."

Think about Columbus who, in the face of general assumptions about the earth's shape, sailed off to see for himself — extended his **self** out there. Columbus would not have proved to everyone that the earth was round and that new lands existed if he had stayed at home in safe, comfortable Portugal and applied for easy duty. A resume could have landed him a steady job in shipping and trading, sailing the same old seas, and he would have been bored. No challenge. No risk. No fulfillment. Ho-hum.

Think about yourself. As you learn and apply New Way skills, you will participate in your own discovery process, and you will be amazed and energized at what you learn about Christopher's round world and the possibilities it holds for you. Your New Way search could open up new worlds for you, just as it has for many Career-Makers graduates.

Job Search Truth #2: Whatever you believe to be the truth about the job market probably isn't.

Developing the skill of extending is critical because you probably know very little about the world beyond your own boundaries. If you go to work at a company each day, you know a lot about that company. However, you may know precious little about the inner workings of other companies. Yet you have constructed ideas in your head about other companies, or industries, and you believe them to be truth. Most of these "truths" about the job market are not true at all. They are assumptions.

Tough Reality: If you have never done it, you may not have the vaguest idea what it is like to show up to work at another company in another industry, or to run your own business. You do not know what opportunities exist for you because you have not researched those possibilities—you have not talked with people in a specific way to determine what other options might be available to you.

Tender Reality: We know only about companies, industries and job titles that have been part of our past. This is the truth for all of us. Because we teach life planning and job search skills to people, it does not follow that we know the reality about other companies, industries and job titles. We are ignorant of most of the rest of the work world beyond the boundaries of CareerMakers. And so, it is hazardous to your future and your potential fulfillment to operate on assumptions about the job market. When you do, you cut your - self off from endless opportunity, and you are likely to stay where you are: stuck in an unsatisfying job or an unsatisfying job search.

When do you "un-stuck" yourself? When do you take your **self** seriously and check out the reality of the work world?

When you are sick to death of showing up to your present job, or you are told not to show up, or you feel restless and wonder if there isn't something more exciting out there for you. Or perhaps you are searching for a new job or career now, and you are not making progress.

In any case, you are <u>ready</u> to learn a dynamic, reliable, tested process because you <u>want</u> to move.

TYPICAL QUESTIONS
Q. Do I network in order to get a job?
A. Immediately, no. Ultimately, yes.

Q. What does that mean?
A. It means that, immediately, you are talking to people in a research mode, exploring companies or industries or jobs of interest to you. You do this to make informed decisions about what you want to do next.

Q. Sort of checking things out?
A. Yes. Like doing a survey. That way you learn the reality of companies and industries. You give yourself solid information on

which to make decisions. You are no longer ignorant of what's "out there." You no longer make assumptions about jobs or career fields — you **know.**

Q. O.K. So where's the job?
A. While researching the job market you will contact many people and develop relationships with them. When you decide what you want to do, and let those people know of your decision, they will help you get to the job openings and the people who have the power to hire.

Q. So, ultimately, the people I contact while doing my research will help me get to job openings when I decide what I want?
A. That's how gracious networking works.

Job Search Truth #3: Most jobs that are available this minute are not advertised anywhere. These jobs constitute the "hidden job market." The hidden job market is simply people...you and me...and the networks we build.

Q. Are people really willing to talk about their jobs and companies?
A. Yes, they are. In fact, people are quite gracious and willing to help if you follow the rules of networking.

Q. There are rules?
A. You bet. And you must learn them so you can go about the process in a credible and professional manner.

Q. This sounds like nothing I've ever done before. I feel uncomfortable. Do other people feel this way?
A. Yes. Most people are uneasy with networking when they first hear about it. But most of us have done it successfully before and perfected the skills. We just haven't called it networking.

Q. What do you mean?
A. Suppose you received a check from your Aunt Tillie for $18,000. Her note said that you had to spend it on a new car. You could add to the amount if you wished, but you could not buy a new car for less than the $18,000. Tell me how you would feel about that.

Q. How would I feel? I'd be ecstatic! WOW! I couldn't wait to start looking for the new car.

A. Right. Tell me how you would decide which car to buy.

Q. How would I make my decision? I'd go to the library and read Consumer Reports to research the kinds of cars available. I'd look at ones that excited me, and check out their performance, features and economy. Then I would visit dealerships and kick some tires, collect brochures and ask a lot of questions. I'd drive some cars too. I'd also be on the lookout for the models I liked and talk to owners in parking lots if I could. When I had enough information, I would make my decision and hand over Aunt Tillie's check. Then roar off into the sunset!

A. Yep. You'd be sure you knew what you wanted BEFORE you spent your money. Pretty smart shopping, I'd say. Well, you bring your unique skills and values into the job market — that's your $18,000 — and you want to do the same kind of research to make an informed decision on where to spend your skills and values. **Before** you surrender yourself to a company to do a job, you want to make sure you're getting the right one. So, you research to find the company you want to hire just as you do research to make any major purchase.

Q. Wait a minute. Don't companies hire people?

A. That's the way it was. However, the New Way search allows you to target and go after the job and company you want. When you get it, you have, in effect, hired your company.

Q. That's a whole new way to think about the job search. Pretty exciting! How does it work?

A. By learning the skills of Busybodying, Researching and Generating Job Interviews.

THE BRIDGE METHOD

When you want to make a job or career change — or you have to — you may feel as though you are on the brink of an abyss. You can see the other side, see where you want to be, but you don't know how to get there. Somehow, you need to build a BRIDGE across the abyss. Whereas the BRIDGE method is useful in any life situation that requires additional knowledge to make an informed decision, the focus here is the job search process.

As you study the BRIDGE model on the next page, you will see that three basic steps are involved in the New Way search. They are Busybody, Research and Generate Job Interviews. The three steps together constitute what we call the "art of gracious networking." When undertaken with diligence and tenacity, these three steps take you across the bridge to a new, better, fantastic job — WHEW!

Let's look at each of these steps as a specific career management method. But first . . .

DO YOUR HOMEWORK!

When you have completed your Compass, you will have focus and direction and stay on course. Indeed, your Compass provides the foundation from which to conduct your job search. Without it you will be doing some willy-nilly, hit-and-miss, fragmented search, and the real possibility exists for making bad career decisions.

NEXT: GO TO THE STORE

To do a professional and credible job search, you must be prepared with the tools of the trade.

First, buy a Networking Notebook to keep track of people with whom you do research interviews. The notebook is a three-ring binder that is roughly 7" X 9". Buy paper to fit (5 1/2" X 8 1/2") and a set of dividers. Label dividers with your areas of interest. If you already use an organizer, give thought as to whether you want to incorporate your job search materials into it. Most people find that a separate binder works best.

Even if you are an inveterate computer jock, you need a Net - working Notebook to take with you on research interviews. If you wish to keep track of your network on your computer, much software is available to do so.

Refer to the Networking Notebook Samples in Appendix A for examples of how to set it up for your search.

Buy a calendar, preferably one small enough to fit into the inside pocket of your notebook. It should have sufficient room on each day to write appointments easily. Or, you can use your software to print daily schedules.

Buy personal business cards. Consider them "confetti" and

The *BRIDGE* Model

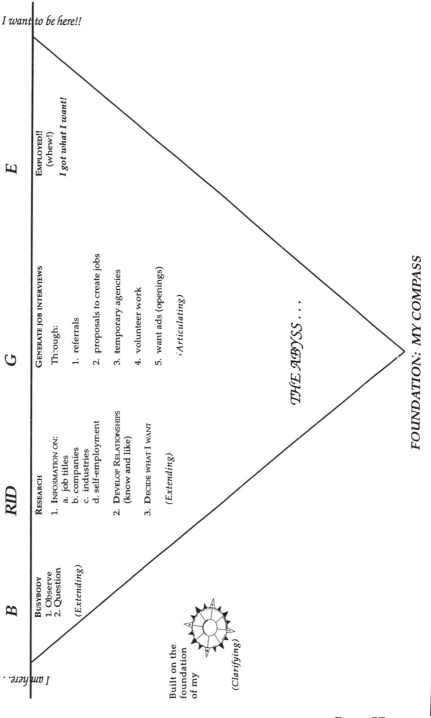

I want to be here!!

B

BUSYBODY
1. Observe
2. Question

(Extending)

RID

RESEARCH
1. INFORMATION ON:
   a. job titles
   b. companies
   c. industries
   d. self-employment

2. DEVELOP RELATIONSHIPS
   (know and like)

3. DECIDE WHAT I WANT

   (Extending)

G

GENERATE JOB INTERVIEWS
Through:
1. referrals
2. proposals to create jobs
3. temporary agencies
4. volunteer work
5. want ads (openings)

(Articulating)

E

EMPLOYED!!
(whew!)
I got what I want!

THE ABYSS . . .

Built on the
foundation
of my

(Clarifying)

I am here . . .

FOUNDATION: MY COMPASS

remember to shower them on those you meet in your job search. Your cards should be printed on decent stock with your name, address, phone and e-mail only. Anything else, except perhaps a general sort of logo, limits you. Your MBA or Ph.D., contrary to what you may think, does not necessarily open up the world to you. It, in fact, may close doors. Your ideal job may not require such a degree, and when people see that you have one, they may dismiss you out of hand. However, if you think your degree might open some doors, get two sets of cards: one with, one without and hand them out appropriately. Confetti cards put you on a horizontal plane with the working world, and allows you to be professional and credible in your search.

Buy a bunch of "thank you" notes. Choose ones that reflect who you are. Make sure you will be comfortable mailing them to people in your network. (More later on how to write them.)

Now you have what you need to do a New Way search and are ready to carry out the three networking steps.

STEP I: Busybody

Job Search Truth #4: The prime rule of the job search is: Open your mouth and talk to people—anyone, anywhere, anytime.

If you look back at the BRIDGE model, you will see that the first step onto the BRIDGE is Busybodying. To take Busybodying seriously is to understand that you don't know where your next job is coming from. However, you do know that you will most likely hear about it from another person. Who? You don't know. That's why it is critical that you do not make judgments about other people, or decide not to talk to someone because he/she is not in your "career field." When you get judgmental, you may not talk to people unless you think they can "do you some good." This is when networking becomes manipulative. In fact, you do not know who can be helpful until **after** you have talked with them. So, you must talk with all kinds of people, everywhere.

Busybodying is a situational activity. You can do it wherever you find yourself: in line at the movies, at cocktail parties, at your child's soccer games. To Busybody effectively, you must simply make an observation on something relevant to the situation, and talk about it. Then proceed with the conversation (or not), depending upon the responsiveness of the other person. You are, in effect, conducting "friendly assaults" on the rest of humanity.

TYPICAL QUESTIONS

Q. Wait a minute! Are you saying that I should strike up a con -
versation with strangers?
A. That's exactly what I'm saying. Remember, your job will come
from and through another person. It could come from the person in
the movie line just as easily as from a company president. It is your
fear and assumption that makethis an unbelievable possibility.

Q. Yeah, well, I'm a "meat and potatoes" person. I like to get down
to business. This Busybodying is silly. How can it have anything to
do with a job search?
A. Busybodying is directly related to the job search in several ways.
It gives you practice talking with all sorts of new people, and this
practice makes you much more at ease during both research and job
interviews. Busybodying also allows you to find openings, and it
helps you expand your network by getting names of people with
whom to do research interviews.

Q. O.K. I see how Busybodying can make it easier to talk with new
people. How does it uncover job leads?
A. Very directly. Here's a true story: A fellow finished   skiing for the day. As he was putting his skis on his car to go
home, he observed another skier doing the same thing. Our
fellow said, "It's a lot more fun taking them off the car to go
skiing than it is putting them on to go home, isn't it?"

Skier: "Yes. That's true, (pause) but I don't have too far to
go home. I live in town up here."

Fellow: "Oh! And what do you do to earn a living?"

Skier: "I'm the director of the museum."

Fellow: "I love that place! Wow! You must enjoy your job."

Skier: "Yes. I do. And what do you do?"

Fellow: "I was caught in the downsizing at the bank. So I'm

doing my research to determine what I want to do next."

Skier: "If you worked at the bank, you must have a financial background."

Fellow: "Yes, I do."

Skier: "Well, I'm going to be hiring a Development Officer. Why don't I put the information about that job in the mail to you?"

Fellow: "That would be terrific! Here's my card."

Q. Pretty convincing, but. . .
A. Look, there are several points to consider here. One is that if our fellow had not opened his mouth and talked to a stranger, he would never have uncovered that possibility. That is the Prime Rule of the job search: **Open your mouth and talk to people**. Secondly, this job was not advertised — remember the "hidden job market?" And, finally, if this "friendly assault" had ended with a job, our fellow would tell his friends, "You won't believe this, but I got my job in the parking lot at the ski resort!" The overriding point of it all is that **he created his own good luck by Busybodying.**

Q. I get it now. So how does Busybodying help to expand my network?
A. First, you strike up a conversation using the observe-comment method. As the conversation progresses, you are usually asked, "And what do you do?"

Q. I know. I hate that question. I'm not "doing" anything if I'm out of work. What do I say?
A. You say the absolute truth, and you say it with enthusiasm: "I'm currently researching corporate training and the food industry. Do you know someone I could talk to in those industries?" More than likely, if there is rapport between the two of you, the person will offer a name or two for you to contact.

Q. Hmmm. Then I call them up and . . .?
A. Take the next step across the BRIDGE (Research). Call for a research interview and begin investigating your interest in training

and food. But do not neglect your Busybodying. Get easy with it. Have fun with it, just as you would if you were buying that new car. See what happens. Learn from mistakes. Don't be judgmental. Make the "wonder factor" central to your search. Ask yourself before you speak, "I wonder what will happen this time?" Then, open your mouth and start creating your own good luck.

STEP II: Research

Job Search Truth #5: There is a structured and directed manner of accessing the hidden job market, and most people don't know how to do it effectively.

Researching is a structured information-gathering process. It is a tool to use for discovering the reality of industries, companies and job titles that sound interesting to you. Also, if you are thinking of going into business for yourself, don't neglect your research. This information gathering process enables you to **make decisions** about what you want to do, and **develop relationships** with people who will come to know and like you. **These people constitute the hidden job market and will ultimately help you find or create your next job!**

The Researching process has definite steps, and you must follow them carefully. If you do not, you stand a good chance of losing credibility. A sloppy job search still gets people to know you. But they sure won't like you much if you become obnoxious or fail to keep in touch, send "thank you notes," or return things.

RESEARCHING STEPS

Here are the basic steps of Researching and, if you follow them, you will conduct a professional and credible job search:
• Identify two areas of interest from your Compass, and people to talk to in those areas of interest.
• Call those people and make a twenty-minute appointment
• Go see them with networking notebook and questions
• Filter your information through your Compass
• **Build your network by keeping in touch with those people!!!**

The following pages explain each step. Read through them to get a comprehensive picture of the research process.

Identify two areas of interest and people to talk to in those interest areas.

Your search should be enjoyable, and it will be if you take your interests seriously. Look at the middle of your Compass and select two areas of interest that you would like to explore, be they industries, companies, job titles or going into business for yourself. These two interests represent the **starting point** of your job search. You can add more interest areas as you progress with your research, but this is where you begin.

If you do not know people in a certain industry, company, or job title, reach out to your friends and acquaintances — relatives, pastors/priests/rabbis, co-workers, neighbors — anyone you already know. Go to those people with whom you are most comfortable, those who are "warm," easy to be with, and ask if they know any - one in your areas of interest. They will, most likely, be able to refer you to people so you can begin your research. Do not discount anyone as a possible "connecter." You might be surprised by who knows whom.

Call those people and make a twenty-minute appointment.

Calling to make research appointments usually causes all sorts of anxiety. It is here that you come face-to-face with your fear of self-promotion. The phone call brings up the negative thinking about the process, and you are likely to resist, avoid and procrastinate. The simple fact is this: resistance, avoidance and procrastination will prevent you from moving along in your exploration. If you do not pick up the phone, you will remain stuck.

To reduce anxiety and make researching appointments, **prepare.** Use the Target Call Sheet in Appendix A. This will help you focus on exactly what you want to say. Before you pick up the phone, write the words you want to say on the sheet.

> "Hello, Mike Green. My name is Jane Thomas. Shirley Quinn suggested I call because I am interested in knowing more about the food industry. Shirley said you have been in the industry for some time and are very knowledgeable about it. I would like to talk with you for about twenty minutes on Tuesday or Thursday morning to get a clearer picture of the industry and your company."

• You have stated what you want clearly and succinctly: information.
• You have stated the boundaries: twenty minutes on Tuesday or Thursday.

Since Mike Green knows Shirley Quinn, he will take your call seriously. Make no mistake about it, Shirley Quinn makes this ap - pointment a reality. Referrals warm up the process considerably and insure success. And, since you are not asking for a job, Mike Green will not feel threatened by your request. In fact, he will pro- bably welcome the opportunity to talk about his industry and his company. (People love to talk about themselves and help others with information.)

If your request for an appointment is denied, it is usually because the person you want to see is genuinely tied up with a project, budgeting, going out of town on business or vacation. Ask if you can call back when things settle down. Also ask if you can talk with someone else in the meantime.

If you call and get voice mail, or Mike Green's secretary answers, simply **stick to your agenda on your Target Call Sheet.** Sec- retaries want information. So, when you hear, "What is this in re- gard to?" follow your script and be prepared to say it twice. After you have said it the first time, the secretary will ask, "What did you say your name was?" That is your signal to start over. Make sure she gets all the information, especially Shirley Quinn's name.

TYPICAL QUESTIONS

Q. Are you telling me to call up perfect strangers again?
A. In a sense, yes. But in each case you have a referral. That is someone who knows the person you are calling. The referral is a link to your contact. You should always be able to say, "So-and-So suggested I call. She/he thought you might be helpful." Your re - ferral insures success in getting the appointment 95 percent of the time.

Q. How do I get started if my friends don't know anyone in my areas of interest?
A. Remember the Prime Rule: Open your mouth and talk to people! You see, when you identify your areas of interest, you enable your- self to become directed in your search. Just tell everyone you see,

"I want to talk to people in the food industry." Then ask, "Do you know anyone I can talk with to find out more about it?"

Q. Will these people give me names?
A. Yes. They will give you names of people to call. People genuinely want to help.

Q. OK. What about secretaries? How can I get past them?
A. There is no way to "get past" the secretary. The only way is **through** the secretary. The secretary is paid to screen callers. Make friends with her/him. Do not state anything but the absolute truth about why you want to see Mike Green. Your conversation will go something like this:

"Hello, my name is Jane Thomas, and I would like to talk with Mike Green."

The secretary says, "And what is this in regard to?"

"Our mutual friend, Shirley Quinn, suggested I call. I would like to talk with Mr. Green for about twenty minutes to learn more about the food industry."

"What did you say your name was?"

"Jane Thomas."

"And you would like twenty minutes of Mr. Green's time?"

"Yes. To learn about the food industry. And it is very impor
-tant that he knows that Shirley Quinn suggested I call."

"I will give him the information and call you back."

"That's great! If I haven't heard from you by Friday (two days from the time of the call), may I call you to see where I stand?"

"Yes. That will be fine."

"Thank you very much!"

And, if you don't get a call back within two days, call to see where your appointment stands. There is not a secretary worthy of the title who will not call you back.

Q. Does it really work like this?
A. Yes, it does. But you won't believe that until you do it.

Q. Any other hints?
A. If you are conducting a full-time job search, make five calls each day to get appointments for research interviews. Five calls do not equate to five appointments. People are very hard to reach. But by making five calls each day, you will always have your interviews scheduled in advance, and you may get past feeling intimidated by the telephone. Five calls a day also means you won't have to make fifteen calls all in one day to get five appointments. That is pure misery. **Phoning is the key to success of your job search.** No calls mean no researching.

Go see them with networking notebook and questions
Do this:
A. Go to your Networking Notebook and **prepare** a page for each person you call. (See Networking Notebook Sample, Appendix A.)
B. **Prepare** your questions in advance. What do you want to know about this person and the industry or company?

BEING THERE
Make sure you spend time developing rapport, or bonding. The person you are asking help from will be more at ease and give you time and information if you talk about your relationship with your referral or anything you might have in common. Take time to do the "small talk." Then restate your purpose in being there and begin asking your questions.

Be aware of your time. You have asked for twenty minutes, so stick to it. You want to be credible and professional, and people are busy. Do not confuse the length of time spent on an information interview with its success. Leave with questions yet to ask...you can always call back.

APPROPRIATE RESEARCH QUESTIONS

The purpose of researching is to find out whether an area of interest is the right fit for you. You know what is important to you in a job if you have thoughtfully completed your Compass. **Your Compass is your guide to formulating research questions**. They should be specific dealing with money/benefits, working conditions/values, people, skills/knowledge. For example, one fellow we know was terminated because he hummed and occasionally whistled as he walked down the hall. In the hall he was not invading anyone's space, so he assumed he could be somewhat noisily happy and not bother anyone. Not so.

When he worked the "people" section of his Compass, it was no surprise that "easy-going" and "appreciative of humor" were the most important characteristics he needed from coworkers to be happy on the job. His research question, based on this knowledge, was:

"Tell me about the kind of people who fit best here. Describe some characteristics that you look for in your employees."

This is an open-ended question, one that cannot be answered with a terse "yes" or "no." These questions usually begin with "How can I....?" or "Tell me about..." or "In your view..." or "What is the procedure for...?" or "What software do you use...?" Questions phrased this way foster discussion, which could give our fellow a pretty good idea of whether or not he would be appreciated.

In addition to your personal Compass questions, here are some re - search questions that are good to ask to just about anyone:

• What issues or challenges are facing this industry and what chal - lenges are facing your company or department? In asking about the industry and the company you get both the macro and micro perspectives. (This kind of question is key to creating a job. See Proposals page 78)
• Tell me about your company's mission statement.
• How is it manifested here? (This gets to work values).
• If I want to know more about this, what publications should I be reading? (People will lend you professional journals and magazines. If you read them with excitement, you are definitely on track with an interest. If they put you to sleep, well...)
• Who else do you recommend I talk with? (This builds your net-

work.)
• If I have any more questions, may I call you? (This gives you permission to develop the relationship.)

Before you go on each research interview, ask yourself what you want to know from this person and formulate several open-ended questions from your Compass. Combine them with a few of the questions above, and you will have your agenda for research in - terviews. **Your questions are not static or boilerplate. You must vary them to get the information you need to make career de - cisions.**

DON'T DO THIS: Never, ever, under any circumstances what- soever — no way— don't even think about it — nope — don't do it —

NEVER TAKE A RESUME ON A RESEARCH INTERVIEW!

Why? Well, you called and made an appointment to **get information.** Presenting a resume at a research interview says, "Yeah. Well. I said I wanted information, but what I really want is a job." A resume is all about **getting a job.** It has no place and serves no purpose whatsoever at a research interview. If you even so much as entertain the thought of sticking one in your networking notebook "just in case," you are confusing researching with getting a job.

The results are disastrous:
•You lose credibility immediately. You asked for one thing on the phone (information). Now you want something else (a job). You do not appear to know what you want or what you are doing.
•As soon as anyone has your resume, it is difficult, if not im - possible, to continue to develop a relationship. The only question you can ask of those who possess your resume is, "Do you have any openings?" The answer is always, "Gee. No. We don't." Click. This means you are not building a network.

What do you do with those "old way" people who expect you to have a resume with you? State quite truthfully, "I'm currently in the research stage of my search, gathering information on your industry (company or job title). The information you give me today will help with my career decisions. I honestly don't know whether or not your industry is a fit for me. That's why I want to ask you some questions about it. Let's get going!" When you say that, you convey that you know exactly why you are there and what you want. In short, you know what you are doing, and you are in control — **credibility plus!!!**

IT AIN'T ABOUT YOU!

When you are conducting a research interview, the 80/20 principle applies. You are there to **get** information not **give** it. Therefore, you talk 20 percent of the time—ask questions, and the other person talks 80 percent of the time— answers your questions. Most job seekers make the mistakes of:
• Having weak or irrelevant questions prepared.
• Talking about themselves and their backgrounds.
• Taking a resume along.

AT THE RESEARCH INTERVIEW
•Enter smiling. Extend your hand and say, "I'm Jane Thomas and I want to thank you for making time to see me."

• After developing rapport/bonding, say, "I have prepared several questions to ask you today." **This puts you in control.**

• Ask if you can take notes. Open your networking notebook, find Mike Green's page and your questions, and ask away!

• Keep track of time. Check in at about 15 minutes by saying, "We've been talking for fifteen minutes, and I have a few more questions for you. We'd better move along."

• At the end of your time together, if you would like referrals, ask**, "Who else would you suggest I talk with?"**

• Wind it up by saying, "Thank you for your time and referrals. **If I have further questions, may I call you?"**

•Collect a business card from Mike Green and offer him one of

Page 68

your confetti cards. Tape his card to his page in your networking notebook. As you become familiar with this process, you will begin to realize that you are in complete control. **You** make the call. **You** prepare the agenda for the meeting. **You** take responsibility for keeping to task and time. **You** end the interview.

WRITE A 'THANK YOU' NOTE

Write a "thank you" note within 48 hours of your appointment. Make it meaningful. Use this simple three-paragraph approach:

•Say something like, "Thank you for taking time to meet with me yesterday. I was surprised that we shared a love of photography. Shirley didn't mention that to me."

•State **something specific** that you learned from the interview. Let Mike Green know that you were listening. This tells him that his time was well spent. For example, "I found your views on working out of your home to be particularly helpful. In fact, in light of your experience I am rethinking whether or not going solo is for me. It does, indeed, seem to be a mixed bag...a lot of freedom on the one hand, and a lot of isolation on the other. I'm sure my meetings with Sally and Bill will clarify the issue for me."

•The only way that people can come to like you is through repeated contact. In this last paragraph of your note, tell Mike Green that you will **keep in touch**. Speak of referrals, "I'll let you know what I learn from Sally and Bill." Or, "I'll call as I have more questions." Remember this about saying "Thanks." The people who see you are operating out of a generosity of spirit. **They will expect the same from you.** Saying thanks is your way of returning kindness to those who are gracious enough to help you with your research. Besides, people love to get "thank you" notes. They put them on their desks or bookshelves and think of you whenever they glance at them. We believe that the "thank you" is the most important piece of paper in the job search because it is so powerful in developing relationships.

The best notes are those that are handwritten rather than typed. Handwritten notes are of a more personal, warm nature. Since you are developing relationships with people, the warm touch with "thank you" notes is preferable to the "business" approach. Select notes you like — that reflect who you are. Then you will enjoy sending them out.

If email is now a constant in your life, think hard before using it exclusively in this process. Again, you want to develop relationships. We suggest that after an information interview you definitely send a handwritten "thank you." Then determine if it is appropriate to continue contact with email. If so, then do it. How - ever, if the people with whom you are meeting are not into technology, follow up with phone calls and notes.

FILTER YOUR INFORMATION THROUGH YOUR COMPASS
What do you do with the information that you gather? Filter it through your Compass, which contains the essentials of what you want in a job. Sit down with your Compass and get reflective and analytical about what you have learned and how it relates to what you want.

Filtering Questions: Ask yourself the following questions and write the answers in your networking notebook:
• What did I learn about the industry or company or job?
• What specific challenges or issues will be faced in the next year?
• Am I intrigued by them? Why? Why not?
• How excited am I by the prospect of working in this industry or company or job? Use a scale of 1-10.
• How does what I learned fit with my Compass: Skills, Interests, People, Working Conditions, etc.
• Could I write a proposal to create work?
• What conclusions can I draw at this point? What are my next steps with this person? How do I keep in touch?

It is necessary to do this filtering exercise to make sense of the information you are gathering. If you do not, your information will be forgotten after you have done several research interviews, and you will feel as though you are not making any progress with your search. This is very demoralizing and leads people to say, "Yeah. I did some research interviews, but they didn't get me anywhere." **It is through this thoughtful filtering that you enable yourself to analyze and strategize what you need to do to keep moving in the process. It is disastrous to skip it.**

Page 70

KEEP IN TOUCH WITH THOSE PEOPLE!!!

**Job Search Truth #6: People hire people they know and like —
whether or not they have the exact experience, background or
skills to do the job.**

The simple fact is this: to be liked requires repeated contact.
Would you refer someone for a job interview that you met once for
twenty minutes? Probably not because your credibility is at stake.
Your job is to create opportunities to re-contact those with whom
you conduct research interviews.

You might be afraid of being a pest, but if you keep your repeated
contacts brief, people won't be put off. In fact, we recommend that
when you talk with people on the phone you tell them how long the
conversation will take. For example, the call might take 90 seconds
or ten minutes. If it's ten minutes or so always ask if this is a good
time to talk. If not, get a time to call back at their convenience.

Build relationships with people you genuinely like. Do not think
you have to cultivate relationships with those who have power and
influence. When and if you need access to powerful and influential
people, those with whom you have developed relationships while
researching will help you get in touch with them.

Methods for Keeping In Touch

• Call and thank people for referrals. This is a 90-second call and
  could be the best thing that happens to someone all day:

  "Hello, Mike. This is Jane Thomas with a 90-second call. I want
  to thank you for referring me to Sally Peters. We me yesterday,
  and I learned a lot. She's a warm and helpful person."

• Call and ask additional questions. The more people you talk with,
  the more questions you raise. Don't be bashful. Call and get the
  information you need to make decisions. Remember, you already
  asked if you could call with additional questions at the end of
  your research interviews.

• Go to the mail. People love to get mail that is hand-addressed.
  Send things of interest, such as cartoons, or articles you think a
  person would like. Always include your confetti card.

• Return things. You asked about publications. Often people will lend you materials to read. Return them with a "Thank You." If there are things you would like to discuss, make another appointment.

• Determine sounding boards. As relationships grow and develop, identify people with whom you have rapport. Because they have a genuine interest in helping, they are easy to call. Coffee, lunch or dinner is an option now. And, given the chance, people will act as mentors or advisors.

• When keeping in touch with people, do so within the bounds of the job search. As you get to know people, you could well move out of job search boundaries into areas of sociability.

• One thing to remember: People will develop a true curiosity about you and your search. They will watch your activities with interest, and wonder where you will end up. And so, the worst question anyone can ask about you is,"Whatever happened to Jane Thomas?" If this question is being asked about you, you are not conducting an effective search — you're simply not networking.

YOUR TRAIL OF CREDIBILITY

When you diligently follow the steps of researching, you will leave a trail of credibility. You will be conducting a professional search. People will respect and admire you. This is important because **the way you conduct your job search is the way you are perceived as a prospective employee:**

• When you call people back and thank them for referrals, you exhibit follow-through and assertiveness.

• When you send a "thank you" you exhibit sincerity.

• When you appear for your research interview with a networking notebook, business cards and specific questions, you exhibit preparedness and professionalism.

• When you call and ask additional questions, you exhibit persistence.

- Through the search, you are showing people that you are thoughtful and competent — you know what you're doing.
- **You project characteristics of commitment and enthusiasm, and people have no trouble referring you to openings and interviews.**

TYPICAL QUESTIONS

Q. There's a whole lot more to this networking process than I thought. I'm overwhelmed. Do other people feel this way?

A. This kind of thorough networking process is new to most people. When they are first exposed to it, they feel overwhelmed. It is a lot to assimilate, especially when most people know so little about networking in the first place. The fact of the matter is, **people simply do not know how to network effectively.** It takes commitment, courage, energy and organization. Most of all, you must follow ALL the steps presented here.

Q. I can see that. It seems to me that it will take a long time to get to the other side of that abyss. How long does it take to do all this research, make a decision and get the job?

A. Here's an answer you don't want to hear. How long it takes depends upon you and exactly how much commitment you bring to your job search. We know you must talk to a minimum of six people in each area of interest to gather enough information to make solid career decisions. But think about it. If you were to get serious and talk to six people a week, in 10 weeks you could talk to 60 people in your areas of interest. When is the last time you talked with that many people to define what you want to do and where you want to do it?

Q. Never. It sounds like a lot of work though. Are you absolutely sure my ideal job won't appear in the Sunday paper or on the Internet?

A. I'm 96 percent positive. And, yes, extending yourself into the world requires hard work. But, it's also fun if you stick to your interests. Look at your job search as an adventure. Then pick up the phone and begin the process. Your energy level and enthusiasm will soar as you begin talking to people in your areas of interest. You will come alive as you get out and talk to people. You will, undoubtedly, uncover possibilities you didn't know existed.

Q. I can see that. I must admit that this is getting interesting. Is there a final word on the process?

A. The final word is this: there is no short-cutting the process. If you just go see people, and write "thank you" notes, you are not networking. You must filter your information, keep in touch and build your network. You must develop relationships. Only then will you create a gracious network of people who will come to know you, like you and, ultimately, help you get the work you want...be it a job in a company, or going into business for yourself, tele-commuting, full-time or part-time work or piecing several different jobs /projects together to make a living.

Q. I see. What's next?

A. Making decisions.

DECIDING WHAT YOU WANT TO DO

The researching process enables you to decide what you want to do. It is important to understand that you may uncover more than one possibility. Therefore, do not think in terms of "**it**." Think in terms of "**them**." As you go about your New Way search, you will find yourself thinking things like, "Hmm. I could do this. I could do that." This is your clue that the process is working. You are thoughtful about your research. You are analyzing, sorting, discarding and keeping information that will help you decide what's next. That's using your left brain.

What about your emotional side? Your right brain? That's where your enthusiasm lives. What is grabbing your insides? When are you saying, "Boy! It would be fun to show up and do that"? Questions like these put you in touch with your true interests and passions — that which puts a "fire in your belly." Don't deny your right brain. Explore every single possibility to work in a field that really excites you. Pay attention to the fire; take your belly seriously.

After talking with people in your areas of interest, you may say, "Wow! I would love to work in this company." Or, you may decide "Phooey! I don't want to do that job." Because your information comes from people who are working in your area of interest, your decisions are based on reality, not assumption. You are making informed decisions.

WHEN YOUR DECISION IS "PHOOEY!"

Let's get back to an earlier example involving Mike Green and the food industry. After talking with Mike and about a half-dozen others related to the industry, you decide this is not for you. You just aren't excited about it. Your skills and values aren't in sync, meaning what you've learned about it just doesn't fit your Compass closely enough for you to be happy. You now have a clear picture of the reality of the food industry and — **Phooey!**

MAKE THE DECLARATION

Call those who have been gracious enough to take time to talk with you and tell them your decision. Your conversation sounds something like this:

"Hello, Mike. This is Jane Thomas."

"Hi, Jane. How is the research going?"

"It's going well. In fact, I have just made a major decision, and I want you to know about it. Do you have a minute to talk?

"Yes. This is a good time."

"Well, as you know, I have been talking with a variety of people in the food industry. Based on the information I've gathered, I've decided that your industry isn't a fit for me. It feels good to know that. I want to thank you for your help. I couldn't have made the decision without you."

"Really. Why isn't it a fit?"

"For several reasons...I learned that there are areas of specific knowledge that I lack for which I would have to go to school. I don't want to go to school to learn chemistry, marketing and nutrition. So, I have decided to pursue my interest in food in my own kitchen."

"Well, that makes sense. What ARE you going to do?"
"As a matter of fact, I'm currently exploring corporate

Page 75

training and computer sales. I'll just bet you know some people I could talk to who are doing those things."

"You don't give up, do you? Well, as it happens, my sister is in corporate training at First Bank. She will probably talk with you. As for computer sales, no one comes to mind right now. I'll think about that. Now let me give you my sister's number."

"Thanks."

"You're welcome. To tell the truth, I can't wait to see where you end up!"

When you share your decision with those in your network, you let them know where you are in the process. It also allows you to continue your networking.

When your decision is "WOW!"
It's time to start the job interviewing process.

STEP III: Generate Job Interviews
You have completed your Step II research enough to know what you want to do. It is time to get into the job interviewing or proposal writing process with companies in your targeted areas of interest. There are five basic ways to do this:

Generate job interviews through referrals
After talking with a dozen or so people in the food industry, you find that it's a match. You thoroughly enjoy being in industry-related companies. You like the environment. You see how your skills fit. You are very excited about the possibility of showing up to work in the industry or company. You are thinking, **"WOW! I'd love to be involved in this!"**

Make The Declaration
Call those who have been gracious enough to take time to talk with you and share your decision. Your conversation sounds something like this:

"Hello, Mike. This is Jane Thomas."

"Hi, Jane. How is the job search going?"

"It's going well. In fact, I have just made a major decision, and I want you to know about it. Do you have a minute to talk?"

"Yes. This is a good time."

"Well, as you know, I have been talking with a variety of people in the food industry, and I've decided that the industry is a good fit for me. Not only can I make a contribution with my skills, I am very excited about the prospect of doing that. The purpose of this call is to tell you that **I'm now ready to get a job.** I hope you will keep me in mind, and if you have any openings or hear of any through your industry network, please let me know.

"I will keep you in mind. But, what exactly do you want to do?"

"My research leads me to believe that I would be terrific in customer service. In fact, I've put some of my related skills on paper. Would you mind taking a look and letting me know if I'm on track here? I don't want to fool myself. How about coffee one day next week?"

"Sure. Thursday morning is good for me...about 10:00."

"That's good for me too. I'll meet you at your office and we'll go from there."

"Great."

In other words, you let the people with whom you have developed relationships know that you now want a job. The paper on which you have written your related skills is really two pieces of 8 1/2" by 11" with four abbreviated skill stories on each page. The conversation at coffee is now 80 percent about you and what you bring to the table in customer service in the food industry. Mike Green already knows you and likes you...now he knows what you want to do, and he will have no trouble referring you to job openings. Please note: we are not talking about a resume at this time. We are talking about skill stories.

If you have done a dozen or more research interviews, and you follow up in this way, **you now have a dozen or more people in your industry of choice who know you, like you and know what you want.** That means that all of these people are helping you get your job. You are not doing this alone! It is probably just a matter of time until you land a job you enjoy in an industry that excites you.

Write proposals to generate job interviews

Job Search Truth #7: Tell me how you will make me money, save me money or save me time, and I will seriously consider you as a candidate for a position in my company—whether or not I have an opening.

There are several applications of proposal-writing in the job/career transition process. First of all, more and more companies are hiring people to work on contract for specific projects. This work climate provides opportunity to market your skills to those companies. Proposal-writing is the way to do that.

Another application is to rewrite your job description within your present company if you like the company, but are not happy with the skills you are using on the job.

Last, we have learned that by far the easiest way to effect a radical career transition is by writing a proposal. You first develop rapport through the research step. By the time you present your proposal, you are a known quantity. In this situation, people don't care what you've done in the past because your proposal shows so clearly what you can contribute in the future. They are willing to take you on knowing that you need to learn new things.

Whether you are using this strategy to create project work, redefine your current job, or make a radical career shift, you must follow the steps outlined here to be effective.

Research - again!

The only way to write a proposal to create a job is by doing re-

Page 78

search. If you are redefining your current job description, you know challenges/needs and you know the players because you have worked there for a period of time. This is your research. If you are looking for project work or a radical career change, the key question to ask at a research interview is, "What issues or challenges will your company be dealing with in the next year?" The answer allows you to begin thinking of how you might help meet those challenges. Match the "inside" information that you gather through researching to your Compass. If you are excited by the match, you are on your way to creating a brand new job.

Realistically, uncovering such possibilities may take more than one conversation. If the rapport is there, this won't be a problem. In fact, savvy employers will be interested in ideas that will make money, save money or save time...which is what your proposal is all about.

The Proposal Format

Using the information you have gathered, you need to show, in focused terms, how your abilities will bring added value to the company. You need to present a strong and clear case. To put your proposal in clear and concise terms, think about what you will do, how you will do it and the results the company can expect when you are hired.

Get Thoughtful:

What will you do to help this person or company with issues or challenges?

How will you carry out what you want to do for the company? Clearly write the steps you will take to meet your objective(s).

Results: If you are given the opportunity to make the contribution, what bottom-line results will the company see? How will you make money for the company, save it money, or save it time (which is money)? In the employer's words, "Why should I say 'yes' to your proposal? Why should I hire you? What's in it for me?" The What. How.Wow! format provides the clarity and succinctness that busy people appreciate.

Now, sit down with the information, blank sheets of paper (or at your computer). Make three columns with the headings:

What I Will Do   How I Will Do It   Results

Length of Proposal
Your proposal should be short. Excluding cover letter and resume, the proposal itself should be not more than four pages. The same rules apply to proposals as apply to resumes...bullets, white space, short paragraphs, bold-faced type. Make it as easy as possible to read.

Research is the key to writing short proposals, because the more you know the less you write. When you do not have enough information, you feel duty-bound to make sure that you cover every possible contingency and write too much that no one wants to read. When you do thorough research, you know precisely what needs to be addressed.

Assemble Your Proposal
After you have roughed out a proposal, you must put it in "deliverable" form. This means you must:
•Have someone proof the proposal for clarity, grammar, and spelling.
•Write a cover letter that tells why you have written the proposal.
•Include a resume supporting your abilities to do what you have proposed — if appropriate.
•Copy your proposal on good quality paper, and have a spiral spine put on at the print shop.
•Assemble your proposal:
      1) Cover letter
      2) Proposal
      3) Resume, when appropriate.

NEVER MAIL YOUR PROPOSAL BECAUSE YOU LOSE CONTROL

Presenting your proposal: Arrange your own job interview
Call the person to whom you will present the proposal.
You should have let him/her know earlier that you were "putting some ideas down on paper" so that this call will not come as a surprise. Remember, you have developed the relationship already, so this should be an easy and exciting call to make.

Your conversation will sound something like this:
"Hello, Mike. This is Jane."

"Hello, Jane. How are you?"

"Actually, I'm terrific! I have finished putting my ideas on paper concerning the challenges you're facing and need about 45 minutes to share them with you. Any afternoon next week would be good for me."

"OK. How about Tuesday at 1:30?"

"Great! I'll see you then. Is there anyone else who might be there? If so, I'll bring additional copies."

"Yes, I'd like Anne to sit in with us. You might bring a copy for her."

"I'll do that. See you Tuesday!"

"I'm looking forward to it."

When you present your proposal, you will be talking with someone you already know and who already knows you. You will also know about the company, its environment and the people who work there. You will know how your skills, values and interests fit with the organization. Your proposal, then, is your job description.

The power in the proposal process lies in your ability to **write your own job description** and **arrange your own job interview.** This is possible only through the methods of the New Way search.

Expectations
Do not expect to be hired on the spot when you present your proposal. Your first presentation will let people know what you can do for them, how you will do it and the results expected if they hire you. But, as familiar as your proposal is to you (you have lived, eaten and breathed it), it's all new to the people at the presentation. They need time to think about new ideas.

After discussing your proposal, ask what "next steps" need to be taken. Or, "Where do we go from here?" Before you leave, make sure you have either a date to meet again or a day on which you call for another meeting. **This is how you stay in control of the situation.** Do not leave saying, "I look forward to hearing from you." If you do that, you give your control away.

Yes , but . . .

There are a couple of fears about proposal writing that need to be addressed. The first one is about money. When you suggest writing a proposal to create a job you may hear, "...a good idea, but we don't have the money to do that." **Write the proposal anyway.** If you are on track with the needs of the company, the powers that be will find the money for the position. This is what usually happens.

What if you write a proposal and they have someone else implement it? Not likely. If they had someone to do it, that someone would be doing it. But, it is a chance you take. However, if you don't write the proposal, you will never know whether or not it would have worked.

Our advice: write the proposal, and if it is not well received for whatever reason, accept that graciously and go on to the next possibility.

SEE PROPOSAL SAMPLES: APPENDIX B

Generate Job Interviews through temporary agencies

Temporary agencies provide opportunities for earning money, doing research, and becoming known and liked. As a matter of fact, more companies today use temporary help than ever before. This is because things need to get done, and rather than hire someone as an employee and pay salary and benefits, temps are hired. And, many companies use temporary help so they can screen people for "temp-to-direct" hiring. That means there are openings, and rather than expend the time, energy and money on a help-wanted campaign, they can actually see how compatible the worker is with the company. You might want to sign on with several temporary agencies while doing your job search. If you do, remember that people hire people they know and like. This applies to temporary staffing as well. Don't sign on and **wait** to be called. Develop relationships with the folks at the agency. Show that you are eager to get going. They will take you seriously and tap **you** for temporary jobs rather than

Page 82

someone who just signs on and fades away.

In order to use temporary agencies as an integral part of your job search, identify several companies you would like to research. Then call temporary agencies and ask specifically if they staff the com - panies you want to research. If so, sign on! Or, call the companies that interest you and ask which, if any, temporary agencies they use. Then sign on with those agencies and request to be placed in those companies.

Once you are working inside the company, identify people with whom you want to do research interviews, call them, go see them and ask your questions. It is probably best to ask for some time be- fore work, after work or on break time. Also, while inside the com- pany you can busybody with coworkers and learn much about the company from them.

All in all, temporary agencies can provide excellent access to finding how closely a company fits your Compass, and you're get- ting paid to do your research!

What about generating job interviews? Well, if you do a good job and people come to like you, you will be asked to apply for per- manent jobs as they become available. In fact, many companies prefer this hiring approach to making blind judgment calls from cold resumes.

Generate job interviews through volunteering

Of course, there's no pay for volunteering. However, if you are not working, you have some time on your hands. Why not take this opportunity to give something back to your community? By setting aside a certain number of hours to volunteer, you give something back and you put structure into your week. (This is something full- time job seekers need desperately: structure.) So, if you volunteer at the zoo six hours per week on Monday and Wednesday mornings, you have somewhere to go at specific times, and you can plan your research interviews around those times.

Aside from structure, while you are volunteering at the zoo people are coming to know you and like you. If an opening occurs and it is in line with what you want, you will probably be invited to interview for it. Many of our graduates have landed jobs they love through volunteering.

Internships, both paid and unpaid, afford similar opportunities. You are on the inside working and learning and having people come to know you and like you. You are in an excellent position to find a need and write a proposal to create your job. And, being on the inside, you will find out about openings.

Generate job interviews through want ads, etc.

Anything that puts you in touch with openings and requires a resume and/or application submitted to someone who doesn't know you and whom you don't know falls into the Old Way, want-ad category. For example:

- •Want ads
- •Job hotlines at companies
- •Employment agencies
- •Recruiters/Headhunters
- •Internal postings at companies
- •"Help Wanted" signs
- •Internet posted openings

This is the least effective way to generate job interviews. In fact, many jobs are listed in these places as a last resort. If someone within the company could have been tapped for the position, it would be filled. If someone from outside the company had been referred for an interview and hired, the position would be filled. There would be no need to place an ad, use an employment agency, or any of the other Old Way channels.

How is it possible to come to know and like you from a few pieces of paper that usually illustrate your past job history? And, if you have the necessary "qualifications" for the job opening and your resume speaks to those qualifications, so does every other resume in the stack. They are all basically the same! How in the world do personnel screeners or hiring managers make decisions on whom to interview?

They use a process of deselection. Anyone who is not a specific, cookie-cutter fit for the position is not considered.

Let's say that you fit the mold and are called for an interview. If you have not done Step II research on the company or industry, how informed are you? How can you even minimally prepare for the interview from a base of ignorance? How can you possibly come across as enthusiastic and dynamic when you are operating from a void of uncertainty?

Should you forget about responding to Old Way openings? Well,

Page 84

if you are serious about getting a job, you will use every method available to you. However, every time you put a resume in the mail in response to an ad, picture it going into a black hole. Assume you will never hear a thing from that black hole — and get on with your research interviews.

TYPICAL QUESTIONS

Q. If I do a New Way search, I'm really in control from beginning to end, aren't I?
A. Yes, you are. You are operating from a base of extraordinary personal power. You are competent. You no longer wait for things to happen so you can react. You make things happen. You become your own careermaker. Once you know the process, it becomes a way of life, and you realize that you can change jobs anytime you want to. You feel at peace with yourself and confident in the process.

Q. It seems you're saying that the BRIDGE method moves people out of helplessness and dependency. Isn't it like kicking the habit of the old way to find a job?
A. Exactly.

Q. Whew! This is exciting and it makes sense. How come I'm feeling so uneasy . . . scared?
A. It's hard to do things in new and different ways. You must stretch out of your comfort zone. In this case, you stretch right out into the abyss.

Q. Boy! I guess! I'm trapped between knowing and doing. If I choose not to do the New Way search, I choose helplessness and unfulfillment. I stay stuck, don't I?
A. Yes.

Q. Any hints on taking the first tiny step onto the BRIDGE?
A. The first tiny step onto the BRIDGE must be preceded by a giant leap.
Q. A what?
A. A giant leap — of faith.

Q. Oh. Have I been hoodwinked into something?

A. Not at all. It's just that as you embark upon this process, it is helpful to sort out your beliefs about people and how the world works.

Q. I'm not clear on this. What do you mean?
A. Take time to think about your basic beliefs.

BASIC BELIEFS RELATED TO THE BRIDGE METHOD

First of all, ask yourself what you believe about what's fair. How do you feel when you hear that someone got a job because he or she knew the people who had the power to hire? After all, there were all those other "qualified" candidates who diligently did all the paperwork to get an interview, and they were barely considered. Does this upset you? If so, you might want to adjust your thinking, because you are buying into the belief that the Old Way resumes, want ads, human resource departments works. You might believe that only those who are most qualified get the jobs. This is not reality, whether or not you think it's fair.

Secondly, what is your basic belief about you? Do you care enough about yourself to feel deserving of satisfying work? Do you feel you deserve fulfillment from a job? If not, you might want to adjust your thinking. You are worthy, but if you don't feel that you are, you will not project a positive image.

Finally, how responsive do you think people will be to you as you conduct your search? Do you believe people want to help you toward a new job? Or do you view people as Scrooge-like and unwilling to talk with you? Do you believe that since "time is money" people will not want to see you for twenty minutes? Do you believe that it's a "dog-eat-dog" world in which you must make it on your own, or not at all? If you believe that humanity is fundamentally unkind, you might want to adjust your thinking. This belief will prevent you from taking your first step onto the BRIDGE. Who wants to pick up the phone and start the researching process with the belief that people don't care and won't help?

If, indeed, these are your basic beliefs about the world and the people who inhabit it, but you have the overriding suspicion that the BRIDGE method just might work, test it. Make the leap. Call people. Go see them. Say "thanks." You will, without a doubt, be

grace

continues to inspire:

it is seen in the generous

helping hands

given in response to specific requests.

— maryanne radmacher —

pleasantly surprised.

On the other hand, if you believe in the generosity of humanity, **you already have made the leap.** You may be uneasy and scared, but it is simply because the process is new to you and you don't want to make mistakes. No one does. However, if you believe people will treat you kindly — even if you don't do it quite right at first — you will pick up the phone.

The belief in generosity means you feel that most people respond to others with grace and compassion. And so, you believe that when you extend yourself, you will be met with grace and compassion. It is this generosity of spirit on the part of others that graciously allows for your mistakes and wishes you well. You see, tapping into the hidden job market means tapping into the enormous reservoir of generosity found in people.

Take the plunge! The water's warm!

HIGH-FLYING RICH
Upon getting his exciting job, Rich emailed an account of his path across the BRIDGE:

I just got my dream job! Actually, it's better than that. I am the new Sales and Marketing Manager for HiTek Kit Airplanes. There was a little bit of 'old way' stuff involved too.

When I did a research interview with Sal's Aircraft, they liked me but said I needed to experience actually building one of their airplane kits to do the job they needed done. I didn't want to do that, so they suggested I contact HiTek Kits. I then made an assumption: I thought if I needed technical expertise to work for Sal's, there's no way a little outfit like HiTek could use me. So, I didn't follow up. (A lesson learned here, believe me.) I took a job like my old one selling equipment leasing.

Soon after, I happened to flip through the Sunday classifieds and spotted HiTek's ad for a sales and marketing person. My work experience had nothing to do with aviation, so instead of a resume, I wrote a letter liberally laced with skill stories and the names of folks I had met in aviation doing my New Way research.

They called me, and we had a great phone conversation. This was followed by three meetings and a trip through their facility. I was then asked to write a marketing plan (my job description).

Here I am! Ten days after the first conversation. This is soooooo cool! CareerMakers needs one of our planes. You still have time to order before Christmas.

Gratefully,

Rich

target your resume... ask questions.

Spice it up

know your reader.

research!

write your stories

Chapter 4

HOW TO WRITE SKILLS-ALIGNED RESUMES

OLD WAY

Chronological
- Believe "one-size-fits-all"
- Dates...no gaps!
- Past companies
- Past job titles
- Duties and Responsibilities
- References Available Upon Request
- Must be one page
- Assume this resume will be appropriate for all openings

NEW WAY

Skills-Aligned
- Know where and to whom resume is going
- Targeted skill stories
- Targeted trait stories
- "Value Added" statement
- References
- Short work history
- Might be two pages
- Know this resume is appropriate for one specific opening

RESUMES: OLD WAY

As an Old Way person you think, "I want a new job, so I better write my resume." Then you spend many angst-producing hours in the quest to write the perfect resume—the one that will land the job. You incorrectly assume that one resume will fit all situations. That resume is sent off, with a great deal of pride and hope, to want ads, and you wait to be called for interviews. After all, it is the perfect resume.

You get very little, if any, response and no requests for interviews. Then you begin to wonder what's wrong with you. Well, the only thing that is wrong with you is that you do not understand the purpose of the resume in a job search.

RESUMES: NEW WAY

First of all, a resume will not land a job. That's not its purpose. Its purpose is to market you into an interview by illustrating how you will be an asset in a specific position — sort of a preview of coming attractions. Ask yourself these questions as you are writing a resume: Where is this resume going? Who will receive it? What does that person want to see? How can I present myself as bringing added value to this situation? If you can't answer these questions, your resume will not market you well at all, because the simple truth is that the effectiveness of any resume is in the eye of the beholder. Therefore, what really matters is that your resume be in sync with what the interviewer wants to see. And, what he/she wants to see is that you have the interest, personality and transferable skills to do the job.

Tough Reality: A resume in a job search is much like a lethal weapon: if you do not know how to handle it properly, it will blow up in your face. Strong statement? You bet. Haven't you become excited when someone asked for your resume? Didn't you take that as a signal that the job was just around the corner? Weren't you thrilled? You slaved over that resume, made it PERFECT and handed it over...and at that moment you lost control. You put yourself in the position of having to call to see if there were any open-ings yet. The answer is always negative and, after the third call, you stop calling. Doors shut. Relationship dead.

When someone asks for your resume saying they want to "circulate" it, you had better think twice before handing it over. There are people who clearly understand that having your resume means they can brush you off.

Remember that relationships are crucial in the job search. People hire people they know and like, and well more than 70% of jobs are filled through word of mouth. **You do not want to shut down relationships; you want to build them**! Be cautious when parting with your resume. Ask yourself, "If this person has my resume, will I be able to develop (or continue) a relationship?" If the answer is no, say, "I'd rather wait until you have an opening because then I can write a targeted resume." Then you can continue to develop the relationship.

Therefore, if you prepare a resume at the beginning of your job search, that resume will drive your job search. You are destined to

Page 92

spend most of your time in the Old Way job search, going through ads and sending your resume to strangers who do not know you. This applies to the Internet as well. After several weeks of no responses, you begin to feel terrible, perhaps even panicky. And, if you are thinking of changing careers, your chronological resume will not market you into a new future. It will keep you stuck in your past. You see no hope of doing anything else.

All of this leads us to state that a resume is, generally, a constraining, constricting piece of paper that closes more doors than it opens.

Tender Reality: You are much bigger than any resume you can write. Why be constrained by one? If you can relax and give up those stereotypical notions of the resume as the be-all and end-all in a job search, **you can open many new doors in many new career fields.**

Job Search Truth #8: You do not need a resume to do a job search.

In the New Way search, you do not write resumes until you have done your research. That is why we say that you do not need a resume to do a job search. The New Way search is **first** about finding out what's out there in your areas of interest that fits your Compass. Then, when you make the decision to generate job interviews in your interest areas, you might need a resume to become a viable candidate to interview for a position.

And, you might not. You may develop such good rapport with your prospective employer that he/she simply invites you come to work. This happens quite often. Larger companies may need your resume to satisfy a human resource requirement that sounds something like, "It's company policy that every employee has a resume on file." In which case, if you are asked for a resume, you could be writing it for the human resource file. Your resume is simply a formality because the person who has the power to hire has requested you for the position.

Whatever the case, from the New Way perspective, any resume that you write should illustrate transferable skills and experiences that are aligned with a particular position. Your resume is then targeted to that position and is not as effective in any other situation.

RESUME AVAILABLE UPON SPECIAL REQUEST ONLY

You know you're cookin' when people refer you to openings. Being referred to an opening means that you will have a conversation with someone at the company who will be able to tell you about the hiring process. While there are many variations on hiring processes, the conversation will probably go something like this:

"Hello, Bill Black. This is Jane Thomas. I believe you're expecting my call. Shirley Quinn referred me to you. I understand you have an opening for a marketing person at XYZ Imported Foods."

"Oh, Jane. I'm glad you called. Yes, we are looking for someone, and Shirley said you were interested in working in the food industry."

"That's right! I've done much research on the industry and have a clear idea that I want to do marketing. What is your hiring process?"

"First, I'd like to see a resume. And, we can set up an interview time."

"Fine. What are the most important skills that you want in the person you hire?"

"Well, we need someone who can function as part of a team doing marketing, problem solving and leading."

"Thank you. That information allows me to target my resume to your position. I'll drop it off tomorrow afternoon."

"That's great. We'll be interviewing on Monday of next week. Would you like morning or afternoon?"

"I'm at my best around 11:00. How's that for you?"

"Fine. I'll see you then if I don't see you tomorrow."

There you are! You have a request to produce a resume for a speci-

Page 94

fic opening. You are definitely a viable candidate. And, when you design your resume using skill stories to illustrate the exact skills that are needed, your resume is tailor-made for that position. When the hiring person beholds it, she is very impressed because most candidates submit a "one-size-fits-all." How refreshing (and comforting) to see a resume that speaks directly to what is needed on this job!

A skills-aligned resume makes practical use of your skill stories. Your stories present your unique background as it applies to the opening because no one has your exact stories. In addition to being targeted to the position, this kind of resume gives people in-sights into who you are. That's why your story file is so important. The more stories in your file, the easier it is to write your resume... without angst.

COVER LETTERS

You almost always need to write a cover letter to accompany your resume. We recommend a simple three-paragraph model that you can use for every cover letter you write. If you use this model, you will end the misery of trying to come up with a new format for each letter.

Paragraph 1: Say why you are sending your resume. In the New Way search it is usually because someone referred you to an opening, or someone you know has requested your resume to interview you for a specific position. Old Way reasons to send a resume have to do with responding to want ads, job hotlines, Internet listings... all stranger-to-stranger conditions.

Paragraph 2: This is the longest paragraph in the cover letter. In it write additional information in the form of skills, traits, experiences that are related to the job, but not found on your resume. Use the story format and indent your stories using bullets.

Paragraph 3: This is the "keep control" paragraph. Indicate that you will get in touch to find out about the interviewing process and see where you stand. Of course, this is much easier to do in the New Way job search because the reader is someone who is truly interested and wants to talk with you.

SPICE IT UP!

When CareerMakers graduates ask us to edit a resume, we are regularly amazed at the discontinuity between the people we know to be energetic and talented human beings and the picture they present on paper. This discrepancy is brought about by a reluctance to toot our own horn, and a fear of alienating the reader. In our quest to please, we reduce ourselves to a common denominator of bland and flavorless, and fade into the rest of the crowd.

Your stories provide spice. "Oh," says the reader, "This one actually gives specific examples of the skills I'm looking for. And, she's not afraid to use a little humor." In other words, instead of inspiring thoughts of a nap, your resume keeps the reader awake.

You know your resume is boring when **you** don't like it. Try including some engaging stories to spice it up and separate yourself from the crowd. Give the reader something distinctive.

TYPICAL QUESTIONS

Q. That's nice, but it can't work like this all the time. There will be other situations when I need a resume fast and I can't ask the questions. What then?
A. Let's be clear: it should work like this most of the time. The effort put into building your network will bring referrals. And, it should be pretty easy to ask the questions. Any other situation casts you into Old Way operating.

Q. So, it comes back to doing the research, doesn't it?
A. Absolutely. The more you know, the easier it is to target a resume to a position. Ignorance causes angst.

Q. Yes, but...there could be those situations that require a resume and I can't do the research. What then?
A. You do the best with what little you know about the position, understanding that the chance of your resume producing an interview is just about nonexistent.

Q. Do I use stories on that resume? Or, would it be better to go to the chronological format? What do they want?
A. My question exactly. I don't know what "they" want, because there is no "they." That resume is going to be routed to a <u>person</u>. In this situation, you take your best shot. You might combine stories

Page 96

with chronology. Or, you might write a skills-aligned resume. Or, you might go with the chronological. Whatever you do, you're flying blind.

Q. Why is this so frustrating?
A. Because we have put so much emphasis on the RESUME (Music up! Lights soft! Angels appear!) as the embodiment of THE WAY to get the next job. It isn't.

Q. What about all those resume books?
A. Most are Old Way in belief. They believe a resume is the way to a job and that their format is best to produce your perfect resume. You can spend a lot of time sorting through the 100 or so books on resume-writing in your local bookstore, making yourself crazy trying to figure out which "onc-size-fits-all" format will work for you. More angst. Forget it. Go talk to people. Write a targeted resume when you're asked for one.

Q. Are you saying none of those books is any good?
A. Some are very good, and we are fond of Yana Parker's books on writing your *Damn Good Resume*. Her books provide many variations on the resume theme that will help you spice yours up. Our basic message is that time spent in front of your PC or MAC composing a resume to go everywhere is a waste of time when you could be out building your network. Here is an example of a cover letter and a skills-aligned resume.

SAMPLE COVER LETTER: THREE PARAGRAPHS

Bill Black
Vice-president
XYZ Imported Foods
2738 N Steiner St.
Portland, OR 90453

Dear Mr. Black,

Based on our conversation, I have targeted my resume as closely as possible to your marketing position. After talking with you, I called Shirley to thank her for connecting us, and she told me that you swim a lap or two several times a week. Perhaps our paths have crossed at the pool, because I am also a swimmer.

In addition to my resume, here are some experiences as they relate to your position:

 ◆Lead a branch field operation by hiring, training and supervising up to 30 employees at a time.
 Result: My sales territory grew in a declining market.
 ◆Maintained an average of 25 cold calls per day in person and on the phone to market my catering business.
 Result: Business grew 20% in second year.
 ◆Researched food/catering market before starting my business. Began business with "eyes wide open" clearly understanding challenges before me.
 Result: Although first year was fraught with ups and downs, there were no unexpected surprises.

I look forward to meeting you in person and interviewing for your opening. I'll see you on the 30th at 11:00.

Sincerely,

Jane Thomas

Page 98

SAMPLE SKILLS-ALIGNED RESUME USING STORIES

Jane Thomas
9051 Artesian Way
Lake Oswego, OR 97065
(503) 555-0000

OBJECTIVE: To boost profits for XYZ Imported Foods by contributing my marketing, problem-solving and leadership skills.

ACHIEVEMENTS:

MARKETING
•Implemented a marketing plan for picnics which consisted of direct mail with follow-up calls and personal calls to potential clients. The first year our picnic business increased 25%.

•Established a marketing plan for Signature leasing with bank branches. Conducted seminars for bank personnel educating them to an alternative form of financing. Met company dollar goals ($5 million) within 18 months.

•As manager of newly opened bank branch, developed relationships with local businesses by making personal calls. I obtained over $1,000,000 in deposits in the first six months.

PROBLEM- SOLVING
•Analyzed my catering business to identify profitable areas for growth. Set minimum limits for business, established a COD policy for jobs under $100 and taught staff to say "no" to unprofitable business. According to industry standards, I was in the top 25% based upon net profits.

•Trained catering staff to "think on their feet" and make decisions and follow through on them. Customer complaints were replaced with compliments.

LEADING
•As food chairman of the 1993 Museum Epicurean Experience, I coached 40 volunteers on how to "talk" to food service people which resulted in a 235% increase in participation and the opinion that the food was the best in the history of the event. I was asked to accept the chair in 1994, and I did.

•Lead a team of doctors through a decision-making process and then coordinated all aspects of locating and furnishing new clinic, resulting in happy docs and a $2500 bonus for my good work.

•Rounded up eight friends for international dinners to be held at each other's homes on a rotating basis. Each month's meal was of a specific national "flavor" and we prepared and brought dishes to share. In the four years that the group met, we learned a considerable amount about Italian, French, Thai, German and African foods (to name a few) and had a lot of fun.

On an 8 1/2 x 11 paper this would be the first page of your skills-aligned resume.

Jane Thomas
(503)555-0000

VALUE-ADDED:
My ability to interact well with others has been one of the secrets of success in my past business ventures. I have always been marketing oriented beginning with my newspaper route (*The Oregonian)* when I was twelve. Within two years, I was the top producer of new subscriptions in Portland.

VOLUNTEER   Museum Epicurean Experience
ACTIVITIES   1992 General Chair
                                    1993-94 Food Chair
                                    Northwest Caterers' Society
                                    1989 Co-founder and Vice-president

EDUCATION:

BS, Liberal Arts, University of Oregon
American Institute of Banking
Projecto Linguistico Francesco deMaroquain

WORK HISTORY:
                                    Bank of the Northwest (503) 555-5555
                                    Superior Catering (503) 555-5555
                                    Jane's Catering (503)-555-5555

REFERENCES   MaryLou Jones
                                President , Superior Catering
                                8876 NW Standard
                                Portland, Oregon 96654
                                (503) 555-5555

                                John Smith
                                VP Finance, Northwest Bank
                                296 Canterbury
                                Portland, OR 96654
                                (503) 555-5555

This constitues the second page of your skills-aligned resume.

ADVANTAGES OF SKILLS-ALIGNED RESUMES

As you review the sample cover letter and skills-aligned resume, please note that there is a mix of stories—both work-related and non-work-related. That is the beauty of the skills-aligned resume: your stories come from your whole life, not just your past work experiences. Also note that, when not tied to chronology, it does not matter when you did what. The last story on the international dinners could have taken place fifteen years ago, as could the banking stories. When they happened doesn't matter. What matters is that you did them.

Look at the structure of the stories. They are condensed versions of longer ones you have written. The second story illustrating the 'Leading' skill has been reduced to:

What: Lead a team of doctors through a decision-making process
How: and then coordinated all aspects of locating and furnishing new clinic,
Wow!: resulting in happy docs and a $2500 bonus for my good work.

Another advantage of this kind of resume is that "gaps" don't matter either. For example, you could not tell from reading this resume that Jane spent six years at home being a full-time mother or that she took two years off to travel the world or that she spent four years working in the hi-tech industry. She can leave out past experiences that do not market her into this situation. She can be very selective in the stories she uses to illustrate her skills.

Can you tell how old Jane is by reading this resume? No.

What are Bill Black's impressions of Jane from this resume? She is engaged in life. She has marketing in her genes...she can't not do it. She has some experience in the food industry through her catering business. She has a passion for food, and knowledge of international dishes which fits with XYZ Imported Foods. She volunteers in her community. She likes to have fun. Shirley likes her. And, she swims!

Bill probably can't wait to interview her.

TOM'S TORMENT

A letter from Tom, a CareerMakers graduate who needed to hire someone, makes our point about resumes:

I find myself talking to myself these days, and I'm not getting any answers. You are to blame.

There is an opening at my company for an experienced estimator. I am reviewing the resumes that have been submitted. The applicants, on paper, run the gamut from the obviously unqualified to those that are apparently well qualified. Education varies from Community College grads to Master degrees in Civil Engineering and math. I have reviewed 38 so far. After the first six I started talking to myself. "Please, resume, tell me what this person's skills are. How did he use these to advantage on the job? What did he accomplish to his personal or employer's benefit?"

I have seen some skills listed. Absolutely zero in accomplishments and no results. I have not seen a resume that even begins to approach the skills-aligned style. They are all the traditional, stilted form that tells nothing about the person.

This is the first time I've had an opportunity to compare "Compass Power" to traditional methods. There is no comparison. The Compass and skill stories are the way to go when seeking new employment. In fact, that's how I landed my job here.

Best wishes for your continuing efforts to help folks!

Very truly yours,

be strong
enough to ask
for what you
want;

have courage
enough to
tell your
stories

Chapter 5

HOW TO CONDUCT JOB INTERVIEWS

OLD WAY
I Don't Know

- I have done no research and I am ignorant of the job and the company.
- Anxiety:
  Interviewer knows me only through my bland "one-size-fits-all" resume.
  I know nothing about the interviewer.
- Confusion:
- Interviewer needs to hire someone. Who are you? Will you fit into the company Do you have the skills to do the job?
- You need information. What does this company do? What is this job about? How do I know whether to say "yes" to an offer? Does this fit my Compass?
- Feelings: ◆Fear ◆Anxiety
- Tension ◆Discomfort
- Frustration

"I just don't know."

NEW WAY
I Do Know

- I have done the research and **I know this fits my Compass!**
- Comfort:
  I have been referred to the opening.
  Based on conversation, interviewer has my skills-aligned, targeted resume.
- Clarity:
  We both know that the purpose of the interview is to see if I am the best candidate for the job.
  I'm prepared to tell stories from my past that illustrate my skills, successes and experiences as they relate to the job, and...
- We both feel free to ask questions.
- Feelings: ◆Comfort
- Curiosity ◆Excitement
- Anticipation ◆Camaraderie

"I sure do want this job!"

JOB INTERVIEWS: OLD WAY

Imagine that you are a hiring manager or a human resource screener. You have a position open, and you are looking through a pile of a hundred or so resumes and cover letters to decide who to call for an interview. You have no knowledge of any of these people who have diligently tried to represent themselves on one or one-and-a-half pieces of paper. You try to be objective, but you find yourself becoming irritated with those who have included personal information, irritated with those who have not written chrono-logical resumes, irritated with those who don't fit your exact re-quirements, irritated with say-nothing cover letters. So, you put all of these irritations into your "NO" stack. Since you know what you like to see in a resume (yes, it's very subjective), your exclusion process is swift and sure. In about ten minutes the pile is reduced to twenty possible candidates. You then carefully review the twenty and select five to interview.

Now, imagine that you are one of the five selected.

Your Phone Rings

"I'd like to speak with John Jones, please."

"This is John."

"John, this is Sue Smith from ACME Resources. You sent your resume to us regarding the position of Marketing Coordinator. We would like to interview you for the position."

"Oh, great! When would you like me to come in?"

"How about tomorrow morning at 10:30?"

"That's fine."

"I look forward to meeting you. Good-bye."

What!?!

You may vaguely remember having sent a resume and cover letter to ACME Resources three or four weeks ago. You vaguely remember the ad, and you look it up in your job search notebook.

Page 106

Yes! There it is! It says:

MARKETING MANAGER

ACME Resources—an environmental
consulting firm needs a person with at least 3 years of
relevant experience as a marketing coordinator.
Will provide support to other area offices. Some
travel required. Send resume to ACME Resources
11310 Harvard Rd., Smithdale, OR 97998.

Now it is your task to prepare for a job interview that takes place in less than 24 hours.What is ACME Resources anyway? What kind of environmental consulting do they do?

What exactly do they mean by "Marketing Coordinator?" Coordinating what? How many offices do they have? What sort of support services do they mean? How much travel is required? What kind of interview will this be? One interviewer? More?

These questions cause ample anxiety and a sense of helplessness. How do you prepare for this kind of interview? Run to the library to see what you can find on ACME? Log on to the Internet to see if ACME has a WEB page? You may find out a few things, but the truth is you are basically ignorant of the company and the job. Because you have such a thin preparation base, you fret and stew and feel as though you're operating in the dark...which you are.

At the interview, the interviewer is trying to find out if you are a fit for the job and whether they like you. You are trying to ascertain the nature of the job and the company to decide how close the position fits your Compass. Hence the confusion, anxiety and tension. If you are offered the job under these conditions, you just don't know enough to make a good decision.

JOB INTERVIEWS: NEW WAY

JobSearch Truth #9: What "they" want is not nearly as important as what you want.

We needed new office space for CareerMakers, so we found a realtor who would help us with the selection process. Our days began to be filled with quick trips around Southwest Portland, dashing in and out of buildings, to see what was available. After exploring fourteen possibilities in two weeks, we were beginning to think we were being too picky: This is too small. This is too big. This has no parking. This is too expensive. This has too few windows. This doesn't feel right. This is run down.

One day in the third week our realtor called and said, "I learned of an opening in a building that I think you'll like." We had heard that before, but once again charged off. When we pulled up to the building, Peter and I signaled each other with tentative smiles and raised eyebrows as we took in the clean parking lot and lovely landscaping, including summer flowers in full bloom. Smiles persisted as we entered the building and found it to be very well maintained. The space available was light with many windows. While not perfect, it could be configured to our needs. And, it would cost less than our present location. It took about ten minutes to make the decision to sign the lease.

Why only ten minutes? Because we had done the research on the other fourteen sites! Based on what we learned from them, we knew that this space not only fit our needs, but that we would love to go to work there every day.

Isn't that why you kick tires and test drive cars? The purchase is easy because, based on your research, you know this is what you want. Isn't that why you date several people before settling on a spouse or partner? The experience of kissing all those toads allows you to learn about your needs and what will make you happy in a relationship. You recognize the prince(ss) almost immediately. The ceremony takes about twenty minutes. In each of these examples, 90 percent of getting to "yes!" was spent doing the research to make sure you knew what you wanted.

It's that way with job interviews. Ninety percent of your effort should be put into research. When an opening comes along, and it fits your Compass, you will be excited about the interview because you know this is what you want. You will gain specific information

Page 108

about the job as you talk with the hiring manager to schedule your interview and, possibly, write your skills-aligned resume. All of this research means that you greatly reduce anxiety on both sides—yours and the interviewer's. In the interview you will be prepared to talk about what <u>you</u> want: how <u>your</u> transferable skills/interests/experiences match the needs of the job.

With New Way techniques, you settle into a job interview under one or more of these conditions:
1) You have been referred by someone in your network.
2) You have already talked with the interviewer.
3) You have been working at the company as a temp.
4) You have been volunteering at the organization.
5) You are presenting a proposal to people you already know
    through your research interviews.
6) You are interviewing for a new position within your present
    company.

You are at this interview because your research has confirmed that this position fits your Compass. You are not talking to a stranger, or strangers. Your networking efforts have placed you in a warm, hospitable environment. In other words, you are there for all the right reasons, and your interviewer is pleased to see you.

SHOW UP, PLEASE!

At CareerMakers each participant conducts two practice video interviews, and we, the staff, evaluate them. What remains common and constant after viewing 7,000 videos is the enormous discon - tinuity between the person we've come to know and love in class and the one that shows up to do the practice video: consistently dynamic, energetic, highly skilled people with fantastic accomplishments become ghostly, hollow, stilted remnants of themselves in an interview situation.

Why is this? First, people do not know how to talk about themselves in ways that convey who they are and what they can do. Secondly, people are so afraid to make a mistake and offend the interviewer that they regularly present their shadowy apparitions rather than their wonderfully human selves. No substance, no pizzazz, no chutzpah, no enthusiasm. Failing to claim their uniqueness and express it, they sell themselves short time and again and wonder why they don't get jobs they know they would like and at which they would excel.

Tough Reality: You probably vanish during job interviews too. Why? It used to be that children were to be seen and not heard. Bragging is frowned upon in our culture. Company cultures emphasize working in teams, and this leads to the use of the pronoun "we" rather than "I." Because of all this cultural indoctrination, and never learning an appropriate way to talk about your accomplishments, you are supremely uncomfortable tooting your own horn... which is exactly what you have to do in an interview.

Tender Reality: You have an abundance of skills, values, traits and interests. If you have completed your Compass you know that. Now, you also have a formula for becoming dynamic and articulate in job interviews: What. How. Wow! With thought and practice you can become your own best advocate without being obnoxious and overbearing. In other words, you can become a skilled interviewee, one who will keep the interviewer awake and engaged.

ARTICULATING IN INTERVIEWS

Learning to tell skill stories in job interviews means that you are responsive to interviewing techniques known as "behavioral focused interviews" and "competency interviewing." Many interviewers use these techniques. You know you are in a behavioral or competency-based interview when your interviewer asks, "Give me an example of when you have used your team management skills effectively." Or, "Give me an example of how you coordinated an event for over 100 people." This means that your task is to come up with an example from your past which illustrates the skill of managing teams and coordinating. "Give me an example" = story.

The interviewer wants specific names, dates, skills and **results**. Why? Because research shows that descriptions of past behavior are fairly good forecasters of future behavior. Your stories describe past behavior. Life history events (stories) are used to determine job skills.

Most of us think we are articulate when we use phrases like, "I'm good with people," or, "I'm a good researcher, " or, "I'm a hard worker." Although these statements sound good, they do not

Page 110

provide concrete information that illustrates the skill or trait and proves the claim. Why should the interviewer assume that those abstract self-descriptions predict good job skills? To become an articulate and dynamic candidate, you must compile a file of stories which illustrates your skills and traits. When you have a job interview coming up, simply go to your story file (see Appendix D) and select the stories you know will best disclose your skills and traits. You will have an idea of which stories are appropriate if you have done your research interviews. When you are invited to interview, ask yourself, What specific skills and experiences should I be prepared to illustrate?

TYPICAL QUESTIONS

Q. You are saying that I should tell stories in a job interview. That sounds rather juvenile and unprofessional, especially if I tell stories that are not work-related. Won't interviewers think I'm frivolous?
A. Aha! Your worst fear: appearing frivolous. No. Interviewers will not think you're silly. They will be delighted that you are so articulate, and that your examples (stories) actually illustrate your ability to do the job. You see, a project management story about designing and building a rocking horse for your grandson could be the one that wins the day and makes you a viable candidate. It shows a very human and warm side of you in addition to illustrating project management skills: you can have fun, you love your grandson, you are imaginative, and you complete projects that you start...you are definitely outcome-oriented, or results-driven. And, no one else can tell that exact story! So, when you fold the rocking horse into the mix of work-related stories, you provide the interviewer with a wonderful, holistic picture of who you are. Remember: people hire people they know and like. Stories make you knowable and likable.

Q. I see that now. How can I get this story process under control?
A. Quit thinking about it and begin writing them. Start your story file, even though it will be a struggle. Then practice telling your stories out loud. It is important to hear your own voice extolling your virtues...over and over again. **Practice! Practice! Practice!** Think of the all the practices and rehearsals that precede performances by professional athletes and entertainers. Pavarotti, Jordan and Streisand didn't become outstanding in their skill and

talent by simply showing up on performance nights.

Q. I get it. How do stories give me an advantage?
A. Other candidates will be groping around in the dark, cobwebby recesses of their minds to dredge up examples. When they think of one, they will not be articulate in the telling...they will ramble on and watch the interviewer slide into a coma. Boring! You will already be prepared, so your responses will be natural, on target and lively. You will not be intimidated. Indeed, you can relax and enjoy the interview. That's the advantage.

Q. What if the interviewer never asks for an example?
A. Your stories will provide you with a solid base from which to operate whether or not you are asked for specific examples. If you find yourself across the desk from an interviewer who does not know how to interview (all too common), just say, "I'd like to tell you about the time I..." and tell a story. In other words, the story preparation stands you in good stead in any interviewing situation.

Q. How do I put this all together for an interview?
A. Study "Bridging the Interviewing Abyss" on the next page. It is a model of interview preparation involving the articulation of your skills, values, interests, and experiences using skill stories. You can use it to prepare for any job interviews that you have in the future.

THE INTERVIEWING ABYSS
Look at the concerns of interviewers. They are afraid of making a mistake and hiring the wrong person. Selecting the wrong candidate causes all sorts of misery. First of all, people have to interact with this mistake every day. Then, the work will not get done. The new employee will have to be terminated, and it costs thousands of dollars to "unhire" a mistake. Next, the hiring process must begin all over again. And, the interviewer loses credibility. Omigod! No wonder interviewers are loaded with anxiety!

Your mission in the interview is to disclose, succinctly and with clarity, who you are, and how your skills and experiences will solve the interviewer's problems. The amount of information you give directly impacts the interviewer's anxiety level: more information means less anxiety.

Bridging The Interviewing Abyss

The BRIDGE: ARTICULATING SKILLS, VALUES, INTERESTS, EXPERIENCE

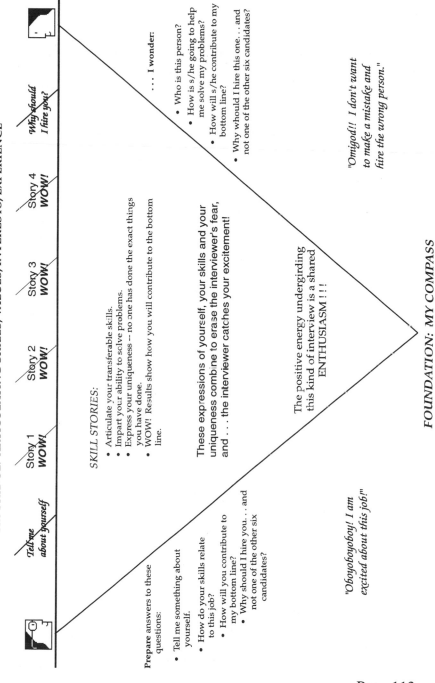

Tell me about yourself

Story 1 **WOW!**

Story 2 **WOW!**

Story 3 **WOW!**

Story 4 **WOW!**

Why should I hire you?

SKILL STORIES:

- Articulate your transferable skills.
- Impart your ability to solve problems.
- Express your uniqueness -- no one has done the exact things you have done.
- WOW! Results show how you will contribute to the bottom line.

These expressions of yourself, your skills and your uniqueness combine to erase the interviewer's fear, and . . . the interviewer catches your excitement!

The positive energy undergirding this kind of interview is a shared ENTHUSIASM ! ! !

Prepare answers to these questions:

- Tell me something about yourself.
- How do your skills relate to this job?
- How will you contribute to my bottom line?
- Why should I hire you . . . and not one of the other six candidates?

. . . I wonder:

- Who is this person?
- How is s/he going to help me solve my problems?
- How will s/he contribute to my bottom line?
- Why would I hire this one . . . and not one of the other six candidates?

"Oboyoboyoboy!! I am excited about this job!"

FOUNDATION: MY COMPASS

"Omigod!! I don't want to make a mistake and hire the wrong person."

Why? Because people hire people they know and like. What can you prepare to **tell the interviewer about yourself** that will be engaging and memorable? Which stories should you prepare to **illustrate your skills** as they relate to the position? **Why should the interviewer hire you** and not one of the other candidates?

If you spend time preparing responses to these three questions, you will be well on your way to reducing the interviewer's anxiety. Let's look at the interview based on these three questions.

PREPARING FOR THE JOB INTERVIEW
Q. TELL ME ABOUT YOURSELF.
Do you groan when you hear this question? Do you think it best to charge through it so that you can get to what really matters? Think again. This question provides you with a platform from which to make yourself memorable and set yourself apart from the rest of the candidates. Forget your past job experience. That's all on your resume anyhow. Talk about your interests. If you restore motorcycles in your spare time, say so. Tell about the one that's in your garage right now, right down to the model and original color. Or, if you travel a lot, say so. Get specific about your favorite trips. If you sing in a barbershop quartet, say so. Describe your group and where you perform and what you like about it. If you enjoy hiking, say so. Then tell specifically which trails you like and why.

Do not recite a list of your interests. That's boring! **Paint word pictures**. Leave the interviewer with memorable snapshots of your interests in his/her head.

Q. HOW DO YOUR SKILLS RELATE TO THIS JOB?
Or, "Tell me how your skills relate to this job." Or, "Give me some examples of how your skills relate to this job." Tell stories. When you have done sufficient research on the company and the job through your research interviews, you enable yourself to "see" how your skills relate. Then, when you are referred to an interview by one of your personal contacts, you can say, "It would be helpful in my preparation if you could tell me the skills and experiences you are looking for in this position." Based on the feedback, you can then go to your story file and find or create appropriate skill stories. It is absolutely imperative that you include results. Results show how you will contribute to the bottom line. They also show that you

are a doer — a person who is able to deliver.

STORY MODEL
Here's the model of how to tell a story (give an example) in a job interview:

DEFINE—	—TELL—	—REALITY CHECK—
the	your	ask a
skill	story	question

Interviewer: Could you give me an example of when you facilitated a relocation?

Candidate: **Define:** To me facilitating means pulling people and materials together to accomplish a task or project. I did this very successfully at ABC Clinic when <u>I facilitated a major relocation for a team of doctors</u>. **(What.)**

The doctors needed more space. That meant either staying where they were and remodeling or moving to a new location.

•I directed the decision-making process, using group processes.
•I researched suitable locations.
•I developed a detailed expense analysis and budget ($200,000).
•I collaborated with the architect and doctors to design the new
  space.
•I researched the pros and cons of custom vs. modular cabinetry.
•I coordinated with the architect, the contractor and the building
 manager to make sure the project stayed within budget. **(How.)**

The results were:
•The doctors were delighted with their new space.
•The doctors received a letter from the building manager stating
 that my close monitoring saved about $10,000.
•I loved developing a plan and driving it through to completion.
•And...I received a $2500 bonus! **(Wow!)**

Reality Check: Is this example in line with the skills needed in this position?

This format provides the interviewer with a clear picture of your facilitation skills, complete with definition, example and reality check! Because **this example can be articulated in about 90 seconds,** the interviewer will not become bored and drift off.

The reality check does two things. First, it engages the interviewer who must react when asked a question. Second, when interviewers realize you are going to ask questions, they pay closer attention to the entire interview. This model enables you to create a conversation for a mutual exchange of information. Most important, you will be heard. When you have mastered this format, you will be an extremely articulate candidate, responsive to today's "behavioral" and "competency-based" interviews.

Q. WHY SHOULD I HIRE YOU...AND NOT ONE OF THE OTHER CANDIDATES? Give trait examples and tell their value to that particular position. Do not use empty clichés of dependability, reliability, trustworthiness without specifics. When you support those words with examples, they are not clichés any longer. Say, "I'm trustworthy. For example, at my last job I was entrusted to balance cash and make a deposit daily. I made no mistakes in over two years, and my average deposit was $5500 per day." This inspires a "wow!" in the interviewer.

WHEN YOU PUT IT ALL TOGETHER...
Here's a short example of the New Way job interview. The situation is that you are interviewing for the position of District Manager for a video rental company. You have talked with a friend, Jim, who is familiar with the company, and you have visited the video stores. Jim has put you in touch with the owner/interviewer. You are excited about the job and are prepared to do self-disclosure...engines ahead FULL!

Interviewer: Tell me about yourself.

Candidate: For years I have been an avid cycler, both bicycles and motorcycles. I have participated in Cycle Oregon for the past three years, and I am looking forward to it this year. I'm a Harley David-son fanatic. In fact, I have one in my garage that I'm restoring. It's a huge project, but I keep at it. I have a picture of the finished pro-duct taped over my workbench...that's what keeps me going. It's a 1960 Harley Panhead and it will be spectacular when it's done.

Page 116

Reality Check: Do you have any interest in cycles?

Interviewer: No, I don't. Although I have admired those who go off on their mountain bikes for long rides. They seem to have a lot of stamina.

Candidate: It does take a lot of training to prepare for something like Cycle Oregon. But the payoff is great! I meet wonderful people, cyclists and townspeople who arrange hospitable greetings and meals along the way. I have to keep focused on that as I'm training, otherwise it becomes sheer drudgery.
    What brings me here today, though, is my interest in movies. I'm a real buff. I see all the new ones as they come out, and rent older ones to view at home. When Jim told me you were looking for a manager for your video stores, I really wanted to interview with you.

Reality Check: Based on our conversation, I understand you're looking for a manager. Is that right?

Interviewer: Well, I'm looking for the right person to manage six video stores. It will take someone who is creative, understands the sales process, and has management experience. Tell me how your skills relate to this job.

Candidate: First of all, I have some direct video store experience. My brother owns Viewpoints, a neighborhood video store in Boston. When I visited him last summer, I spent time at the store and was fascinated with the business.

Interviewer: Oh...what is his inventory?

Candidate: About half of yours at any one store. I've visited each of your stores, and I'm am impressed with the people behind the counters and the selection of videos available. Some of your sales staff have been with you for a long time. That speaks well of you and your ability to find and keep good employees.

Interviewer: Thank you. I'm ready to step out of the day-to-day management role. That's why I'm interviewing people

Candidate: Yes, that's what Jim said. My direct management experience comes from fifteen years with Beta Consumer Finance Co. I supervised fifteen offices and hired all managers and most support personnel. My turnover was consistently among the lowest in the nation.

Interviewer: That's impressive. But, I'd like to hear an example of retail skills that You would bring to the company.

Candidate: Sure. Let me tell you how I brought the "Heyday of Hollywood" to my brother's video store. When I was in Boston for two weeks last summer

• I compiled data on general operations, customer service and video sales and rentals.
• I designed and implemented a computer system on videos and film stars to create immediate access to them, complete with information on availability and location in the store.
• I trained the staff on the system.
• I analyzed and improved in-store customer traffic patterns
• I implemented programs like 99¢ Day and drawings for free videos.
The results were:
• Business boomed! My brother was hiring additional people in four weeks.
• Customers trusted recommendations from the staff, which increased repeat business.
• Employees were involved and proud to be working at the store
• My brother was ecstatic, and he paid me a small bonus, which was completely unexpected.

Reality Check: Am I on track here? Are these the kinds of skills that would be useful in your business?

Interviewer: Absolutely! You obviously enjoyed the challenge, and you have good management skills. I am interviewing several other people for this position. Why should I hire you and not one of the others?

Candidate: You should hire me because I'm not only skilled, but conscientious. <u>For example</u>, when I needed to buy a car a couple of years ago, I made sure I got four-wheel drive. That way I was always the first person at the office on bad-weather days keeping things going until others arrived. Also, I bring enthusiasm to this position. Yes, I loved the challenge in Boston, and I know I would thrive on the challenges presented here. It's because of those challenges that I want this job!

Reality Check: When will you be making your decision?

Interviewer: Probably by the end of next week.

Candidate: May I call you next Friday afternoon to see where I stand?

Interviewer: That would be fine.

KEEPING CONTROL

Who's in control in a job interview? Well, if it is a mutual exchange of information, neither the interviewer nor the candidate controls the interview. It is give and take. Picture a Ping-Pong game. I hit the ball, you return it. I return the ball to you, you hit it back to me. The person who fails to return the ball loses that round. To win a round in the interview situation, you must keep returning the ball. **Every time you do a reality check, you return the ball.** To that extent you have control in guiding the interview. Study the above sample interview and leave out the reality checks. Do you see how much information would be omitted? Opportunities missed to articulate?

In fact, you **give** control to the interviewer by not asking questions. For example, the interviewer asks, "Tell me about yourself." You stop talking after, "It's a 1960 Harley Panhead and it will be spectacular when it's done." Silence. It is now up to the interviewer to proceed to the next question. You failed to return the ball. You have set yourself up to be a reactive, inarticulate participant, rather than a proactive one. How many times have you left a job interview only to beat yourself up for not having asked this or said that? Reality checks will make you feel much better about your interviews, and will also provide you with information that you would not have received as a reactive participant.

Ask for a Follow-up Time

When the interview is over, ask if you can get in touch with the interviewer to learn the outcome of the interviewing process. At the end of the interview ask, "When will you be making your decision?" When you do this, you do not need to sit around for days hoping/wondering/wishing/praying that the company will call. You are in control. You can continue your job search and simply make the call on Friday.

Say "Thanks"

After your job interview, write a letter (or a note, depending on the situation), of thanks to the interviewer. In it express your gratitude at being chosen as a serious candidate for the position. State why you want the job and why you are a good choice. Look to your Compass for information. The company's values might match your work values. The state-of-the-art computer system might be exciting for you. Certainly write about the problems that your skills will solve.

End your letter by stating that you look forward to the next interview or working together, whatever the situation dictates. Make a short (90 second) follow-up call to make sure your letter arrived.

If you have been interviewed by two or three people, send letters or notes to each of them. If you have participated in a panel interview, write to the person in charge.

TYPICAL QUESTIONS:

Q. Yes, but that's the ideal. Get real! Interviews won't always go according to this format. What then?

A. Of course, you're right. Variations on the interview theme include how skilled interviewers are, how open they are to having a conversation, and what the company or organization's procedures are. However, the constant in all of your job interviews is you. Practice and preparation provide you with the means to chart your course through most variations. You can show up confident and articulate whatever the conditions.

Q. OK. But what if I find myself in a situation where I haven't been able to do all the New Way stuff?

A. Again, as with the resume, take your best shot based on what you know. Prepare. Practice. Realize you're probably not a very viable candidate, and be surprised if you're taken seriously for the position. If you are, it's because of your positive self-disclosure and your ability to articulate what you can do for the company.

Q. So, I can't lose if I take myself seriously, put my story file together and practice, practice, practice! Right?
A. Right!

Q. Realistically, aren't there other questions that I should be prepared to answer?
A. Sure. Here are a few of the ever-popular, always-asked questions and some of our perspectives on possible answers.

Q. What are your greatest strengths and weaknesses?
Customize this answer for each interview. Get thoughtful about the job for which you are interviewing. What do you like about it and why? For example, suppose you are excited about a training job, and the interview is coming up.

Q. What is your greatest strength?
A. I'm very good at culling material from a variety of sources and innovative thinking. I have created manuals and designed a CD Rom. I have built strong training programs in the past and have been praised for my results.

Q. What is your greatest weakness?
A. In the training arena, I find that I lose interest in "canned" programs. That is why I'm excited by this job—it allows for creative program development.

Q. Under what circumstances did you leave your last job?
If you have trouble answering this question because you are angry or embarrassed about being terminated or downsized, work on a response (practice out loud) that you like until you are satisfied that you can say it easily. For example:
A. I was caught in the downsizing that the bank did several months ago, along with 80 others.

A. I knew that the new computer system would impact my job. It did, and my job was eliminated.

A. I was fired. My manager and I didn't see eye-to-eye on the effectiveness of the new computer system. Since I couldn't get behind the project, I was asked to leave.

A. I want a job which matches my values more closely, so I chose to leave in order to find it. Based on my research, your company is a great match.

Any of these statements is sufficient. There is no need to embellish your answer with details. If you are not past the anger/embarrassment of being let go from your last job, the telling of details is disastrous simply because your anger shows. That's why practice is important.

Q. What kind of salary are you looking for?

In actuality, this question should not come up at the job interview. It is appropriate to talk about salary when the job is offered. However, sometimes it does come up in interviews inappropriately. It is in your best interest to have the interviewer state a figure first. Therefore, if asked, you might reply:

A. I don't want to under- or overvalue myself. It would be helpful to know what you have budgeted for this position.

A. I would prefer not to base salary for this position on the duties and responsibilities I had at XYZ Company. What is the salary range here at ABC?

A. I've done research on this, and it seems the range for this position Is $_____ to $_____. How does this compare with your range?

A. You know, I've read some of those books on salary negotiation and they all say not to state a figure first, so...what's your range?

A. Are you offering me the job? If so, I'm delighted. What do you have budgeted for the position?

Q. Describe a situation where...

Situation questions seem to be favorites with some interviewers. Common situations involve making professional and personal decisions, handling difficult situations, solving specific problems and working with difficult people. Again, identify some situations from your past that apply, write stories to illustrate them, and practice out

Page 122

loud.

Q. Why do you want to work here?
A. I have conducted 15 research interviews with people in the industry, including three with people in your company. As a result, I know that my values are aligned with your company's. Your culture fits my needs and your employees have the qualities I want in my co-workers. This position and company match my Compass. (This leads to a discussion of your Compass as it relates to the job, letting the interviewer know what you want.)

PANEL INTERVIEWS
Do these things in order to keep your wits about you while interviewing with more than one person:
1) Prepare in the same manner that you would for a one-on-one interview...stories, stories, stories!
2) Shake hands with each person.
3) Get as comfortable as possible in your seat.
4) Make eye contact with each person.
5) Then concentrate on being responsive to whoever is asking the question. Direct your answer to that person. Do reality checks to try to engage the interviewer.
6) In between questions, make eye contact with others.
7) Upon leaving, thank the panel. Shake hands if it seems the appropriate thing to do.

Here's how a New Way panel interview worked: One of our graduates did many research interviews within a state agency and determined that he would really like to work there. Because the people with whom he did this research came to know him and like him, they informed him of an opening for which he should interview. They told him it would be a panel interview. He prepared for it by practicing stories that would be applicable based on all the information he had gathered. When he walked into the interview room, there were six people on the panel, and he knew five of them. His research enabled him to say something of a personal nature to each as he shook their hand. From a final pool of eight candidates, he was selected for the position.
Can you imagine how comfortable he was at the interview? Can you imagine how his very presence reduced the anxiety of the

panel? Can you see the importance of conducting research interviews and developing relationships? And, can you see the difference between New Way and Old Way job interviews? The truth of the matter is, the farther away you are from inside information through friends or research interviews, the farther you are from the job.

HEY! LOOK ME OVER...

An interview provides you with an opportunity to sell yourself. It is important to know exactly what you want to sell and to whom. Your Compass tells you what you want to sell; your research tells you to whom. You must show up to the interview as who you are, because your interviewer(s) will assess, evaluate and judge you... it's human nature. Therefore, you want to make sure you are evaluated for the qualities that are important to you. Present your dynamic, energetic, skilled self at the interview...allow the interviewer(s) to evaluate you on all the right criteria. Then, if you do not get the job, it just wasn't a good fit.

SANDY'S SELF-DISCLOSURE

Sandy, one of our graduates, was referred to an opening in an organization she knew nothing about. She called CareerMakers, and we connected her with another graduate who had written the organization's newsletter. Sandy did a research interview with this graduate. She also went to the organization to get a feel for it and pick up any brochures that were available. In the meantime, she called the contact person within the organization and learned of the skills needed to do the job and was requested to send a resume. She prepared and sent a skills-aligned resume, and called to make an appointment for the interview, which was scheduled for breakfast at a downtown restaurant. Sandy tells it this way:

I really practiced for this interview...yada, yada, yada! Stories, stories, stories! So, I was ready. I took my networking notebook with me, which, of course, has a copy of my Compass right in front. I referred to it from time-to-time to make sure I was staying on true North. Into the interview awhile, my interviewer asked, "What is that?"

"This is my Compass," I said. "It has all the elements I want in a

Page 124

job. I'm referring to it to track how closely your position fits my Compass."

"May I see it?" she asked. "Of course," I said and handed it over. Well, the rest of the interview was driven by my Compass! We both used it as a template to compare to the opening. She asked if she could keep my Compass, and I said, "Sure."

The next week I received a call requesting me to interview with the director of the organization. When I arrived, the director immediately pulled out my Compass! Again, my Compass was the centerpiece of the interview.

I was hired because of the clear self-disclosure that my Compass provided. Wow! Yada, practice, yada, yada, practice, practice, practice! What power...what confidence!

Thanks so much for the insights and tools to make this happen. I'll keep in touch...

Sandy

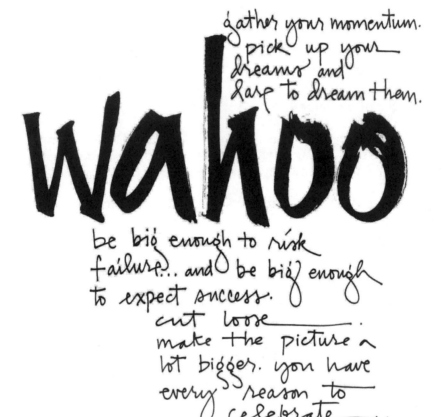

gather your momentum.
pick up your
dreams and
dare to dream them.

wahoo

be big enough to risk
failure... and be big enough
to expect success.
cut loose_____.
make the picture ∧
lot bigger. you have
every reason to
celebrate_____.

— mary anne radmacher —

Chapter 6

How To Manage Your Transition

OLD WAY

- No Compass
- No plan of action or strategy: Trying a variety of hit-and-miss methods
- Isolated —at home with want ads and Internet
- Reactive: Waiting for the phone to ring
- Feeling: Scattered
- Fragmented Depressed
- Powerless Frustrated
- Devalued Angry Fearful

NEW WAY

- Compass completed
- Action Plan in order
- Scheduling and conducting research interviews
- Attending church/temple, association meetings, health club, kids' school stuff and
- Busybodying like mad!
- Taking time for family
- Feeling: Focused and Directed Confident In control Optimistic Good about my ability to market myself into my future

Job Search Truth #10: A successful job search or career transition is 20 percent left brain/analytical (technique, strategy, planning) and 80 percent right-brain/emotional (how you feel about yourself and your ability to relate to the rest of the world).

Our graduates who end up with meaningful work make a plan and put one foot in front of the other to execute it. They are both disciplined and flexible, optimistic and cautious, analytical and emotional. The path to their new work did not run in a nice, tidy, straight line. Instead, it was a path of zigs and zags, hairpin turns and detours. Drawing on their experience, we give you their ten tips on what it takes to "do it"...find work that is, for you, worth doing.

1) Analytical: Do it "by the book." Complete your Compass. Develop your file of stories and practice them out loud. Follow the Seven Rules of Researching to the letter. Put your action plan together. Become disciplined in your approach. Those who have been successful say, "I did what you told me to do." **This is a transition system, and if you omit a part of the system, it simply will not work well.**

2) Emotional: Fear is a constant. Don't let it keep you from doing it. The truth is that much of this is probably new to you. The truth is you do not know how to do research interviews perfectly. The truth is that you are uneasy about calling people. The truth is you probably don't want to do any of this because it looks big and overwhelming and you feel inadequate to the task. The truth is you will make mistakes, and you will learn from them. And, like learning anything new, the truth is that confidence will grow with every call you make, every research interview you do, every story you write.

3) Emotional: Keep the process 'warm' by beginning to research with people you know: your family, friends, co-workers, neighbors, pastors/priests/rabbis. These are the people who will get you started. Ask them who they know in your interest area and to facilitate a connection for you. Get names and telephone numbers. Make appointments! (If you are very isolated and have few friends or family, your first step might be to consider joining an organization or two, including a church or temple. Begin by finding supportive people.)

4) Emotional: Understand that this is a highly emotional process. Your sense of self is challenged hourly. It is true that the better you feel about yourself, the more likely you are to put these methods into practice. If you find that you become panicky and stay stuck, perhaps some emotional/psychological counseling is in order. We regularly recommend such counseling to our clients. In the meantime, you should have some fun and do things that make you feel good about yourself:

•Exercise! • Volunteer your time !• Take classes!• Busybody!
• Spend time with family and friends! • Go fishing!
•Read a novel! • Go to movies! • Get a puppy! • Swim, ski, knit,

build an aquarium, play with the kids, go to the beach, play the piano, chess, poker, basketball, cribbage. • Add your own:

5) Emotional: Unless you are absolutely financially strapped (in which case you should get a job—any job—today!), don't let your current financial situation keep you from doing it. We cannot count the times we've heard the "I can't because..." statements. This rationality can keep you stuck by saying or thinking, "I can't change my job or career. I have mortgage payments and kids' college expenses," or, "Even though I don't like my job, I've got financial security and good retirement benefits, and I don't want to give them up." This is faulty thinking: just because you do the research, it does not follow that you will change your job or career! You decide whether or not to make a change **after** you've done your research. In other words, don't let your rationality mire you in a trough of inertia.

6) Analytical: If you are currently employed, make a commitment to yourself to do one researching interview each week. People will meet with you before work, after work, during lunch, for coffee, and on Saturdays and Sundays. When you feel more comfortable with the process, schedule two or three researching interviews per week. The point is to get going!

Analytical: If you are unemployed, formulate a weekly action plan (See Appendix C). For example, you might commit to a plan that says you will be busy with BRIDGING activities from Monday through Thursday each week, ending at 5:00 on Thursday. During those four days you could conduct six research interviews (Research), attend an association meeting, trade show or career fair (Busybody), and have a job interview (Generate Job Interviews). You should also volunteer your time. Volunteering puts structure in your week and connects you with people who share your interest. So, if you love animals, why not volunteer at the zoo? Old Way activities—responding to want ads in newspapers and on the Internet should occupy about 10% of your time...it's a crapshoot and you have no control in those situations. And, on Thursday at 5:00 you will have accomplished what your plan dictated, and set up your appointments for the next week. Now you can enjoy a long weekend doing things that make you feel good about yourself. This weekly plan puts boundaries to your search. If you do not have boundaries, you will be consumed with the process seven days a week, twenty-four hours a day, and that's not healthy.

7) Emotional: Share with your family what you are doing. Share your Compass, your dreams. Let them know about the researching process and the people with whom you are doing your research interviews. Share what you are learning about yourself and your areas of interest. Make a weekly date to keep people informed, perhaps every Thursday evening at dinner. If you have a standard time to share your transition activities you will actually do what your plan dictates. This weekly date provides you with **personal accountability** while making your family feel included and informed.

8) Emotional: If you are constantly thinking about getting to the end of your transition, you will not enjoy the process on a daily basis. You must concentrate on what you are doing today and tomorrow—one foot in front of the other—and you will get to the end. People want to know how long it will take. It is a highly individual process with infinite variables: what sort of network do you have going into the process? What is your fear factor? Do you need counseling for anger or self-confidence? Would you rather go on a vacation, remodel the bathroom, or spend time relaxing, healing, catching up on reading? For how long? How many research interviews are you going to do per week? How much muscle are you going to put into your search? All of these variables lead us to answer: **it takes as long as it takes.**

9) Emotional: Give yourself credit! Every time you do <u>one thing</u> with regard to your transition, kick up your heels, pat yourself on the back, holler, "Yessssss!" Each thing you do means you are putting one foot in front of the other: formulating your weekly plan, making a call, scheduling an appointment, going to a meeting, writing a story, conducting a research interview, sharing with your family. **Don't ever minimize your efforts.**

10) Emotional: Keep the faith! You won't get that new job/career yesterday, and it probably won't happen today. But it will happen eventually when you quit thinking about it and begin doing it!

TYPICAL QUESTIONS

Q. I had never thought about it before, and I'm surprised at how much emotion is involved in the process. I'm really an analytical person, and I don't think I can change—don't think I want to. What then?

A. We are not suggesting that you change. We want you to be aware of the emotional impact involved in the process so that you will not be blindsided by it. There's no doubt about it: the emotional components either keep you moving or keep you stuck.

Q. How does that work?

A. You know what you need to do, but you don't do it and this makes you feel awful. For example, you know you should be making calls to schedule researching interviews. This is foremost in your mind, yet you spend the entire morning doing laundry and cleaning the garage. Noon arrives and, while you feel OK about the laundry and the garage, you realize that those were avoidance activities. In the meantime, the phone looks huge—like it weighs about 500 pounds. You feel terribly intimidated and stuck. You have let yourself down. It's very easy to get into this spiral, and it's all emotion.

Q. I can see that. And to avoid that spiral...?

A. Focus on the job/career transition activities. That's your job now—not the laundry or the garage. We believe that the busier you are with Busybodying, Researching and Generating Job Interviews, the better you feel. Get your action plan in order and discipline yourself to stick to it. Then you won't let yourself down. You'll feel good about your progress.

Q. Whew! That's a lot to do, isn't it?

A. It seems like a lot because these aren't your usual activities. However, you're actually putting in less time than if you worked a full week. It's an opportunity to fill your days with excitement: exploring things that are of interest to you, making new friends, learning new things, helping others. Your transition will take on a pleasant life and rhythm of its own, and you will be energized by it.

Q. If I need a job now, I can't spend time doing all of this, can I?

A. If you need a job because you are concerned about paying the rent and putting food on the table, you cannot afford to take the time to do the New Way search.

Do a budget so that you know exactly how much money you need to make. Put all your efforts into finding a survival job as soon as possible. Use all means available to get your job including friends, relatives, want ads, Internet. When approaching temporary agencies be sure to develop relationships rather than just "checking in" over the phone. Be positive and professional. Get yourself situated in your survival job and then begin to implement New Way methods so that you ultimately get what you want.

AMY'S AVALANCHE
Amy was climbing Mt. Hood with a team of climbers. Weather conditions on the mountain changed abruptly, causing Amy and three others to be caught in an avalanche. She tumbled 1200 feet down the mountain, pummeled by snow and debris for a seeming eternity. And then she stopped, not knowing which way was up or where she was. Amy survived with a broken pelvis and a broken leg. One person died.

Amy sent these Season's Greetings to CareerMakers:

A year after graduating from CareerMakers, I'm starting to put my life back together. Who would have guessed I'd spend so much time dealing with serious injuries? However, I've told many people that dealing with the physical injuries was nowhere near as difficult as dealing with the process of redefining myself and reentering the work-force after my previous job experience had thoroughly dashed my self-definition. I have to thank you for the progress I've made on these less visible difficulties. Thank you so much for your wisdom, common sense and heart.

Love,
Amy

Amy is saying that job loss and subsequent career transition were emotionally more traumatic than being caught in an avalanche! She is now employed as Research Director of the Sierra Business Council and looks forward to cross-country skiing and snowshoeing this winter.

Page 132

Maybe you have been pummeled by circumstances in your work-life. Perhaps, just now, you don't know which way is up with regard to your life and career. What you have between these covers is our wisdom, common sense and as much heart as it is possible to convey in print. Our sincere hope is that you find here information that will make your transition easier and more effective.

Please feel free to email us with your questions or comments: careers@careermakers.com.

Courage doesn't always roar. Sometimes courage is the quiet voice at the end of the day saying, "i will try again tomorrow."

mary anne radmacher-hershey © 91 c9

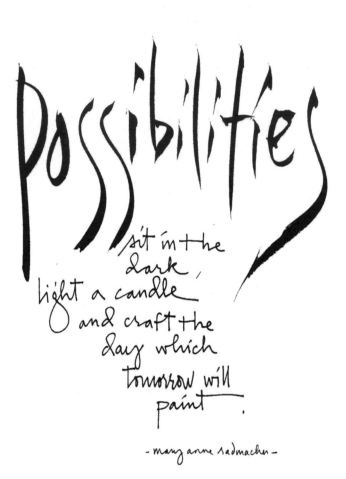

Possibilities

sit in the dark, light a candle and craft the day which tomorrow will paint.

- mary anne radmacher -

APPENDIX A
RESEARCHING/NETWORKING NOTEBOOK

_ Sample TARGET CALL SHEET

_ Sample Networking Notebook page

_ Other suggestions

TARGET CALL SHEET

It is wise to use a Target Call Sheet when making calls to secure appointments for research interviews. Having a script in your hand makes you more confident, because you do not have to grope around for the right words. You always have your script for reference.

person I'm going to call:	Name of person who referred me:	Request: What do I want from this person?
Mike Green ABC Foods 555-7171	Shirley Quinn — Neighbor	HELLO_____ My name is _____ Shirley Quinn suggested I call you because I'm interested in knowing more about the food industry. Shirley said you have been in the industry for some time and are very knowledgeable about it. I would like to talk with you for about twenty minutes-preferably on Tuesday or Thursday morning-to get a clearer picture of the industry in general and your company specifically. Is either of these days good for you?

YOUR RESEARCHING/NETWORKING NOTEBOOK

Here are some suggestions for setting up your notebook. Please adapt as you see fit. The point is to keep track of people and your relationship with them. Even if you choose to use computer database software to keep track of people, you need your notebook when going on your appointments.

Sample Page
Mike Green
ABC Foods
555-7171

Referral: Shirley Quinn
Called 10/18
Appointment 10/27 — research interview 10:30
Mike referred me to Bill Jones - 555-6234 Kate's Catering
              Pat Bell - 545-7651 Gourmet Desserts

Mike's Business Card:

Mike Green, President
ABC Foods
8095 Grant St.
Portland, OR 97665
503-555-5555 Fax 503-555-5555
emai:l green@abcfoods.com

Keep in Touch:
Sent Thank You 10/27
Called and thanked for referral to Bill 11/9 — Voice Mail
Called and thanked for referral to Pat 11/19 — Voice Mail
Called and asked more questions 11/23 — 15 minutes
Sent article on new food distribution system 11/25
Etc...........

Other Suggestions:
   Place a copy of your Compass on the first page of your notebook. This will cause you to be in constant contact with it. Refer to it often. It is also

Page 136

useful when conducting job interviews to stay focused on what <u>you</u> want.

Prepare a page for taking notes while at the interview. Write NOTES at the top of the page.

Prepare a page for answering your Filtering Questions after each research interview. Write FILTERING at the top of the page, or use your computer. Don't neglect this! After several research interviews, you will not remember who said what unless you FILTER.

These are suggestions for keeping track of your network as you build it. Modify as you see fit so that you have a workable system.

APPENDIX B

SAMPLE PROPOSALS
Each sample proposal was successful in obtaining new work.

Each proposal was written after conducting research interviews — sometimes five or six. While you are perusing them, try not to become judgmental and nit-picky, thinking, "Well. That's not enough information." Or, "I would have included this or this." You must remember that **you were not present at the research interviews, and you do not know the players or the situation.** And, that's what proposal-writing is about: people, relationships, needs and specific situations.

Note that the proposals here use What.How.Wow! or Goal (What), Solution (How), and Results (Wow!) to convey, succinctly and with clarity, how the writer will make money for the organization, save money or save time. Every proposal recipient said, "You're on! This is exactly what we need."

Remember the axiom: The more you know, the less you write. You might be amazed at the brevity of these proposals. They are short and right on the bull's eye with <u>the exact information needed</u> because of the research interviews conducted by the writers.

If, right now, you have done the research, know the players and the situation in a certain organization or company, you could be ready to knock their socks off by writing a proposal!

STEVE'S PROPOSAL:
Steve worked for the State in land acquisition. He knew that a certain company was going to get into land acquisition, and that they would need someone who knew the "ins-and-outs" of the acquisition process. Furthermore, Steve saw an opportunity to move from the public sector to the private sector, something he had wanted to do.

After conducting seven research interviews and building relationships within the company, he wrote the following proposal and presented it to the appropriate people. He was hired to develop and direct a land acquisition unit — a much bigger job than he had imagined.

The ( ) parentheses illustrate the use of What.How.Wow! Steve changed those words to Goal, Solution and Benefit because he liked that language better, but wrote his rough draft using W.H.W!

Page 138

COVER LETTER

Norm Last, VP
Jones, Singer & Meyer
3218 SE 19th St.
Portland, OR 97884

Dear Norm,   February 1, 1996

The following pages include the proposal we discussed, followed by my resume.

I believe a significant new market is emerging. With the addition of a land-acquisition unit, Jones, Singer & Meyer would be well positioned to benefit from this opportunity. I am confident that with my extensive experience in this field that I would be the right person to create, launch and manage this unit.

I welcome questions concerning this proposal. Please feel free to contact me.

Sincerely,

Steve Adams
1247 Byer Street
Portland, OR 97812
(503) 990-6673

PROPOSAL FOR CREATING AND MANAGING A LAND-ACQUISITION UNIT AT JONES, SINGER & MEYER

Steve Adams   February 1, 1996

RATIONALE STATEMENT
Cities, counties and other local public agencies (LPA's) rely on the State for trained staff to do land acquisition for their projects.

The State is facing a 3-fold increase in funding for its own projects in the next four years. There is not enough personnel to handle this growth.

Land acquisition is complex and must conform to Federal requirements to assure funding. A new market is emerging for providers who integrate land acquisition with engineering, surveying, planning and construction management. Jones, Singer and Meyer would do well to get into this sort of integrated land acquisition.

GOAL (What I will do)
Design, implement and manage a land-acquisition unit to expand Jones, Singer and Meyer's market share with LPA's, thereby increasing company revenue.

SOLUTION (How I will do it...Steve writes his own job description)
A. Develop and implement a land-acquisition unit at the company in order to:
1. Assist management team in bidding new services to LPA's. Integrate land-acquisition bid with bid for engineering, surveying, construction management services.
2. Provide pre-project estimates of land-acquisition costs to clients. Provide cost comparisons between alternate designs.
3. Appraise value of all property rights to be acquired for a project.
4. Negotiate purchase of all necessary property rights.
5. Clear title.
6. Administer Federal relocation funds and assistance.
7. Comply with all federal regulations to assure funding.
8. Provide land-acquisition expertise to our management team.

B. Manage acquisition unit to:
1. Contract for services as required. Select and oversee contractors.
2. Recommend hiring and training additional staff as required.
3. Expand unit to Jones, Singer & Meyer's offices in other cities as required.

C. Market new services through new and established contacts.

BENEFITS TO JONES, SINGER & MEYERS (Results: Wow!)
By responding to this large new opening in the market, the company will:
1. Increase its ability to bid a wider, well-integrated range of services.
2. Increase its market share.
3. Generate new income. Best estimates indicate a minimum of $500,000 in the first year.

STEVE'S RESUME

This resume illustrates Steve's present job...period. Since the position he is creating with his proposal requires someone who can step in with the exact experience and credentials to do the job, it is unnecessary to write about any other jobs in his work history.

Steve Adams
1247 Byer Street
Portland, OR 97812
(503) 990-6673

WORK EXPERIENCE
State Land Acquisition Agent, 14 years

•Negotiated acquisition of millions of dollars worth of land for highways, parks, greenways, airports, mass transit, from a diverse public throughout the state.
•Achieved unsurpassed success statewide, exceeding 95% within tight deadlines.
•Appraised market value of hundreds of commercial, industrial, agricultural and residential lands and structures.
•Appraised fee value, easements, leases; capitalized income.
•Obtained expert consultation from private providers.
•Consulted for local governments to assure their land acquisitions conformed to federal regulations.
• Assured federal funding.
•Interpreted and administered federal law.
•Conducted public hearings.
•Developed marketing program and sold $600,000 of surplus property.
•Generated significant new cash flows.
•Facilitated relocation of businesses and persons displaced by public projects.

EDUCATION
M.S. 1989, Portland State University
B.S. 1978, Northwestern University

KATHY'S PROPOSAL

Kathy loves pre-schoolers, but she didn't want to work with them full-time. She used New Way methods to find an organization that offered classes to the community. One of her research questions was, "Why don't you offer classes for pre-schoolers?" Most said that they either hadn't thought about it, or that it was too great a liability risk. Kathy persisted until she found the director of a hospital community education program who liked her and her enthusiasm for pre-schoolers.

Kathy wrote a simple proposal, including a cover letter and her resume which showed that she had worked with preschoolers in the past and had an Associate degree in Early Childhood Education. The Wee Walker class was so innovative that *The Oregonian* newspaper wrote an article about it with a half-page picture of Kathy and the children enjoying a walk a-round the neighborhood.

Here is the What.How.Wow! portion of Kathy's proposal. It illustrates how to get paid for something you enjoy rather than volunteering.

PROPOSAL FOR WEE WALKERS CLASS

What I will do:
1. Plan, coordinate and implement a walking program for 3-4 year olds.
2. Make the class available to children Monday and Wednesday morning from 9 a.m. to 10:30 p.m. for nine weeks.

How I will do it:
This program will target two goals for the children:
1. Learning more about their physical ability. Walking as well as body awareness through a variety of movements...hopping, jumping, turning, clapping, etc.
2. Enjoying the process of learning about their outdoor environment... weather, sounds, sights, smells.

Results:
1. Provide a great program for Community participation.
2. Promote health and fitness for children through the hospital's Health and Fitness Center.
3. Fees will cover instructor's wages, and return money to operations.
4. Allow parents two hours off per week while their child is taught in a positive, safe, nurturing setting...time they can spend in the Health and Fitness Center!

SARA'S PROPOSAL

Sara liked her company and the people with whom she worked. However, the company had fallen behind in its use of technology, and she recognized a need to update and enhance computer operations. In fact, she knew that she was the only person in the company (about 30 employees) who had the knowledge and technical expertise to do the upgrading.

As happens many times, Sara had approached her boss with her ideas only to have her boss say, "Yeah, Sara. We do need to do something about that." And then walk away. Of course, nothing got done. Sara felt frustrated, devalued and invisible. When she learned the proposal-writing process, Sara decided to use it immediately. She went to her boss and said, "You know that I've been talking about computer upgrading for a-while. Well, I have put my ideas on paper, and I would like 45 minutes of your time to walk you through them. How about one morning next week?"

Her boss was astonished to think that Sara had not only taken the time to write ideas down, but that she scheduled an appointment to talk about them! Sara was no longer invisible.

Sara's proposal has two parts...a cover letter and her new job description. There is no need for a resume because she is known by her boss. She has written "Objective" for What, "Methods" for How, and kept Results.

SARA'S COVER LETTER

Medical Associates, Inc.
7865 NE Athens
Portland, OR 97555   May 9, 1997

Attention: Board of Directors
           George O'Reilly/Executive Director

Dear Sirs:

I have been with Medical Associates, Inc. for over eleven years now, and in that time I have seen and been part of many changes within the organization. I have come to know and work with most of you. The last three years have been especially exciting and full of challenges with the reorganization of the management team as well as significant operational adjustments and staff reassignment. Everyone has made great contributions to this new direction and I am grateful to have been a part of it.

I believe new opportunities are presenting themselves daily to give us new challenges. With this in mind, I would like to put before you an idea I have put much time and thought into. It is one I believe will greatly benefit M.A.I. in the long term. It would allow you to take advantage of my skills and open the way for creation of a new position and/or department within the organization. I have included with this letter a brief description of goals, objectives and methods for your review. This is by no means a complete and final description. I see an opportunity for ongoing development of the position and expansion of duties relating to the ever-growing needs of our clients.

PROPOSAL

Subject: New Job Title/Description
To: M.A.I. Board of Directors
               M.A.I. Executive Director

From: Sara Behrens

I propose to establish a new job title/description at Medical Associates, Inc. to be identified as Facilities Development and Research Specialist.

Reports to: Executive Director as part of the Administration Team
Goal: On-going development of computer enhancements. Identify and develop solutions to problems encountered in computer operations, both software and hardware, as well as office functions and procedures.Establish resource for clients through extensive research on carrier procedures, contract requirements and reimbursement trends.

New Position Description: Six Specific Functions

Objective: Centralize function of computer operations
Methods: Specialist will <u>focus</u> on existing and anticipated problems and report directly to software vendor to assist in the development of solutions. Establish regular follow-up procedures to facilitate speedy resolutions. Collect and prioritize enhancement requests through committee process. Report directly to software vendor with requests and assist in applications. Write detailed enhancement proposals and problem-solving request reports.
Results: Increase computer efficiency and speed up processing of data both outgoing and internal. Free supervisory staff to focus on team and management issues.

Objective: Utilize database retrieval software (ORIGIN)
Methods: Complete loading of master file information in ORIGIN Library. Willing to get further instruction in this area. Willing to travel to their site.
Results: Allow management to extract our own reports in a format we desire. Extensive statistical gathering potential. Reimbursement guide updates. Better client understanding of reports they get from our office.

Page 146

Objective: Enhance and expand database in existing master files through regular updates.
Methods: Establish condition of existing master files through study of data. Establish regular schedule of input time each day until files are complete.
Results: Speed account processing time by allowing operator access to database exclusively through use of computer CRT.

Objective: Update reference library of manuals with H.M.O/P.P.O participation data
Methods: Research current contract requirements; reimbursement levels and client membership lists. Develop ways to load this information on the computer system.
Results: Accurate, up-to-date information. Better staff resource. Easy access to information.

Objective: Improve reimbursement methods from carriers on pain management claim.
Methods: Meet with represen-
tative of carriers to develop efficient clear reimbursement practices on these claims. Develop pain management specialty in billing and reimbursement.
Results: Clarity. Less likelihood of incorrect application of fund received. Less staff time spent researching proper credit of funds

Objective: Familiarize M.A.I. with major carrier procedures in provider relations arena.
Methods: On a regular basis, go out into the field and meet with key representatives of these carriers. Establish positive business relationships through face-to-face meetings. Communicate our needs to carriers and request that they adapt to those needs. Find out needs of carriers and be ready to adapt our operation to those needs.

VERN'S PROPOSAL

Our last example illustrates the effectiveness of the proposal in making a radical career shift. Vern worked in an extremely high-risk job which took him away from home and his two small daughters most of the time. Vern and his wife made a values-based decision...he would quit his job and find one that would not put him at physical risk and keep him home so they could be a real family. At CareerMakers, Vern decided he would like to research the financial industry and ultimately developed relationships within Baxter Funds, a company that sold financial services — 401 (k) plans and individual mutual funds. He decided he wanted to go to work for this company and knew that his past work life was completely irrelevant in the financial industry.

Vern wrote a three-page proposal with a simple cover sheet which stated: Proposal from Vern Barnes. On the first page he described what he had learned about the small pension market and market opportunity. The second page of the proposal was his job description, and the last page marketed Vern into the position using skills and traits only — no resume. This shows the power of not only knowing your transferable skills and traits, but using them in a practical way in the career-change process.

Vern was hired, even though in his 'past life' he had been a Flight Instructor in the Air Force for F-16's. His new company did not care nearly so much about what he had done in the past; they wanted to know what he would do for them in the future. They took a flyer on him (pardon the pun) because they came to know him and like him through the researching process. Vern has been with the company for several years now.

PART I: THE SMALL PENSION MARKET

A. Market opportunity: Over 600,000 businesses have pensions with plan assets of less than $25 million, and 80% are defined contribution plans.

B. Current Use of Mutual Funds:Small defined contribution plan assets held in mutual funds:

Balanced Mutual Fund	3%
Bond Mutual Fund	3%
Stock Mutual Fund	9%
Money Market Mutual	13%
TOTAL MUTUAL FUND:	28%

C. The Market's Growth Potential
Small plan sponsor activity:
 *Sought new money managers since initiating plans 46%
 *Changed money managers 33%
 *Expect to initiate a new plan within two years:
    21% of Defined Benefit Sponsors
    13% of Defined Contribution Sponsors
 *Planning to convert to another plan type:
    17% of Defined Benefit Sponsors
    13% of Defined Contribution Sponsors

Sales and Marketing
Top two criteria for selecting money manager
1. Performance record selecting a money manager
2. Ongoing support and communication

Top three ways to reach samall construction sponsor decision-maker
1. Favorable articles small defined contribution
2. Executive seminars sponsor decision-makers
3. In-person sales calls

PART II: PROPOSAL

Design and implement a series of programs to increase the 401 (k) market share and individual mutual fund sales.

Goal: Promote use of mutual funds in plan assets.
Solution: Develop an education program explaining the risks and rewards of mutual funds vs. other options. Specifically discuss equity income Funds. Program will target "investors" and "non-investors" and will be ongoing.
Result: Increased sales of Baxter Funds.

Goal: Make it easy for the client to invest.
Solution: Mechanize the 401 (k) process. Explore automatic pension investing options with Data Processing.
Result: "Hassle free" investing for the client.

Goal: Increase efficiency of customer communications.
Solution: Develop the best on-line information possible using technology to resolve incoming calls. Explore more ways to provide customer's requested information. (electronic mail, facsimile)
Result: Increased customer satisfaction and loyalty.

Goal: Increase market share.
Solution: Target businesses changing/adding money managers. Target businesses converting/adding new plans. Hold executive seminars and track In-person sales calls. Sell performance record, ongoing support, and communication. Develop a call-back program for clients who have requested information.
Result: Increased sales of Baxter Funds.

PART III: SKILLS AND TRAITS

Baxter Funds needs someone with (1) leadership, communication, sales and computer **skills**, and (2) the **traits** that make the application of these skills effective.

(1) SKILLS

LEADING Williams AFB Officer of the Year for leadership. Flight leader for combat training missions of up to sixteen aircraft. Supervised a class of student pilots through all aspects of training, receiving excellent feedback on all evaluations.

COMMUNICATING Five years of instructor experience with students of varied backgrounds including international students. Wrote manuals For multi-national air exercises. Selected to present mission results to European Command Headquarters.

SELLING Sold endoscopic surgical equipment to surgeons, nurses and hospital administration. Graduate of a Johnson and Johnson Sales school. Completed three-day sales seminar by D. Forbes Ley.

COMPUTER Proficient with personal computers, including Lotus 1-2-3 and Word. Mainframe experience includes programming orbital Trajectories in FORTRAN and ALGOL, and validating Space Shuttle Programs for NASA. Systems manager for f-16 mission support computer.

(2) TRAITS

RELIABLE Considered "work horse" of my fighter squadron. Completed every task thoroughly.

TEACHABLE Able to quickly learn new subjects. Distinguished graduate from **four** Air Force flight training programs. Intelligent.

ENTHUSIASTIC I take work very seriously while maintaining an open, enthusiastic work environment. Stress goal completion through teamwork. I am self-motivated to continually improve.

APPENDIX C

DOIN' IT....

_ Sample weekly Action Plan

_ Beginning: Identify two interests and specific people to call

_ Your weekly Action Plan

BEGINNING
Begin by identifying two areas you want to explore. Then ask your existing network to connect you with people in those areas of interest. "I'd like to learn more about high tech marketing and car restoration. Who do you know that I might talk to about that?"

TWO INTERESTS:
1.
2.

FIVE PEOPLE:
1.	4.
2.	5.
3.	

These are the first five people I will call and make appointments to see for researching interviews:

When you make these appointments and write them into your action plan (next page), you're doin' it!

MY WEEKDAY ACTION PLAN
Research, Busybody, Generate Job Interviews, Volunteer

CareerMakers Weekly Action Plan
Research, Busybody, Generate Job Interviews

Day	MON	TUES	WED	THU	FRI	SAT	SUN	EVENING	NOTES
8:00									
9:00									
10:00									
11:00									
12:00									
1:00									
2:00									
3:00									
4:00									
5:00									

APPENDIX D

SAMPLE STORY FILE

-Assessing skills and traits

-Adapting stories for skills-aligned resumes

-Adapting stories for job interviews

-Note: Most skills and traits are **bolder.**

ASSESSING SKILLS AND TRAITS: A STORY FROM WORK EXPERIENCE

What I Did: I **facilitated** a major relocation for a team of doctors.

How I Did It:

- I **directed** the decision-making process using group processes.
- I **researched** suitable locations.
- I **developed** a detailed expense analysis and budget ($200,000).
- I **collaborated** with the architect and doctors to custom design the space.
- I **researched** the pros and cons of custom vs modular cabinetry.
- I **coordinated** with the architect, contractor and building manager to stay within budget.
- I **supervised** the move to the new location.

RESULTS = WOW!
- The doctors were delighted with their new space.
- The doctors received a letter from the building manager stating that my close collaboration saved about $10,000.
- I loved developing a plan and driving it through to completion.
- I received a $2500 bonus.

SKILLS (STATED)	TRAITS (IMPLIED)
I can:	**I am:**
—facilitate	—creative
—research	—resourceful
—develop	—reliable
—collaborate	—industrious
—coordinate	—a team-player
—supervise	—goal-oriented
—direct	

ADAPTING STORY FOR SKILLS-ALIGNED RESUME

NOTE THAT THIS STORY ILLUSTRATES TWO SKILLS. ALWAYS USE THE STORY FORMAT.

THE SKILL: FACILITATING

(What) I **facilitated** a major relocation for a team of doctors
(How) By researching new locations, developing a budget, collaborating with the architect, building manager and tradespeople,
(Wow!) ultimately saving the doctors $10,000 and receiving a $2500 bonus.

IT LOOKS LIKE THIS ON YOUR RESUME:

I **facilitated** a major relocation for a team of doctors by researching new locations, developing a budget, collaborating with the architect, building manager and tradespeople, ultimately saving the doctors $10,000 and receiving a $2500 bonus.

THE SKILL: COLLABORATING

I **collaborated** with architects, a building manager and tradespeople to facilitate a major relocation for a team of doctors, saving $10,000 and receiving a $2500 bonus for my good work.

ADAPTING STORY FOR JOB INTERVIEW

My research into your position leads me to believe that **facilitating** skills would be beneficial to you. Is that right?

What: Several years ago I **facilitated** a major relocation for a team of doctors.

How: I **researched** suitable location I **developed** a detailed expense analysis and budget ($200,000) I **collaborated** with the architect and doctors to custom design the space. I **researched** the pros and cons of custom vs modular cabinetry. I **communicated** and **coordinated** with the contractor, architect, building. manager and tradespeople to stay within budget.

The results were (say this out loud every time):
The doctors loved their new space. I enjoyed facilitating the process and driving it through to completion. The doctors received a letter from the building manager stating that my close collaboration saved about $10,000. And...I received a $2500 bonus!

Reality checks (use one or all):
Do you think that this example illustrates my ability to facilitate projects? Is this example in line with what's needed in this position?

Adapt story to illustrate the skill of collaborating.

WHY SHOULD I HIRE YOU? ADAPT YOUR STORY TO ILLUSTRATE A TRAIT

You should hire me because I'm **goal-oriented**. I facilitated the major relocation of a team of doctors by collaborating with the architect, building manager, tradespeople and contractor until the new space was perfect and the move was completed. In the process, I saved the doctors about $10,000 and was so effective they gave me a $2500 bonus. I'm sure you want people on your staff who can get results like this. Right?

ASSESSING SKILLS AND TRAITS: A STORY FROM VOLUNTEER WORK

What I did: I **built teams** that more than doubled my neighborhood's donations to the American Cancer Society.

How I did it:
- I **recruited** 50 people from a specific geographic area, telephoning from a list provided by the A.C.S.
- I **conducted** a meeting with these people and **educated** them to the mission of the organization and risks of cancer, using up-to-date materials and a guest lecturer.
- I **facilitated** role-play situations so that participants could practice asking for donations.
- I **divided** the group into ten local neighborhood teams.
- I **provided information** for them to read and **scheduled** a meeting for each team.
- I **finalized** details at team meetings and **instructed** member sin the handling of money collected and the proper way to organize paperwork.

RESULTS = WOW!!
1. My teams collected almost $12,000—more than double last year's donations.
2. I received an award from the A.C.S. for outstanding service.
3. I enjoyed building my teams.
4. Many of the people in the teams became my friends.
5. I was proud of my efforts and gained much personal satisfaction from their results.

SKILLS (STATED)	**TRAITS (IMPLIED)**
I can:	**I am:**
—build teams	—hard-working
—conduct	—resourceful
—facilitate	—dedicated
—instruct	—caring
—recruit	—enthusiastic
—provide information	—persuasive
—educate	

Page 158

ADAPTING STORY FOR SKILLS-ALIGNED RESUME

NOTE THAT THIS STORY ILLUSTRATES SEVERAL SKILLS. ALWAYS USE THE STORY FORMAT:

THE SKILL: TEAM-BUILDING
(What) I **built teams** to solicit donations for the American Cancer Society,
(How) by recruiting 50 people, educating them to cancer risks and facilitating role-playing to ask for donations.
(Wow!) My teams doubled donations to almost $12,000.

IT LOOKS LIKE THIS ON YOUR RESUME:
I **built teams** to solicit donations for the American Cancer Society, recruiting 50 people, educating them to the risks of cancer and facilitating role-playing to ask for donations. My teams doubled donations to $12,000.

THE SKILL: RECRUITING
I **recruited** 50 people to solicit donations for the American Cancer Society by persuading them to attend a meeting, educating them to the risks of breast cancer and training them to ask for donations. My teams doubled donations to $12,000.

THE SKILL: EDUCATING
I **educated** 50 people to the risks of cancer by using up-to-date materials and a guest lecturer. When soliciting funds for the American Cancer Society, these people doubled neighborhood donations to $12,000.

ADAPTING STORY FOR JOB INTERVIEW:

Based on the research I've done on your position, it seems to me that you need someone who can **build teams** effectively. Is that right?

What: Let me tell you about the time I **built teams** that more than doubled my neighborhood's donations to the American Cancer Society.

How: I **recruited** 50 people by telephoning from a list provided by the A.C.S. I then **conducted** a meeting with these people to educate them to the mission of the organization using up-to-date materials and a guest lecturer. I **facilitated** role-play situations so that participants could practice asking for donations. I then **divided** the group into ten local teams and sent them home with materials to read. I **scheduled** a meeting with each team to finalize details regarding handling the money collected.

The results were (say this out loud every time):
My teams collected $12,000—more than double last year's donations. The teams thoroughly enjoyed the camaraderie and training. I loved building my teams and was proud of their results.

Reality checks (use one or all):
Is this example in line with the **team-building skills** needed in your position? Would you like to hear more details of this? I believe this example illustrates my ability to **build teams**. Don't you?

Adapt story to illustrate the skills of recruiting or training.

WHY SHOULD I HIRE YOU? ADAPT YOUR STORY TO ILLUSTRATE A TRAIT:
You should hire me because I'm **dedicated**. As a volunteer, I once recruited 50 people to raise money for the American Cancer Society. I educated and trained them and supervised their canvassing for donations. My teams raised $12,000 and I received an award for outstanding service. I'm sure you're looking for that kind of **dedication** from the person you hire. Am I right?

ASSESSING SKILLS AND TRAITS: A PERSONAL STORY

What I Did: I relentlessly pursued and ultimately fixed a major mechanical problem with my aging Honda Prelude.

How I Did It: This car would quit running intermittently and just not start. This left me stranded on several occasions, so...

- I **assessed** the nature of the problem, **examined** and **tested** several possibilities and **concluded** that something was wrong with the electrical system, and took the car to a mechanic.
- After having my car towed four times in the month it was "fixed" by the mechanic, **I decided to experiment** on my own.
- I **copied** relevant pages of my repair manual, sent them to my father and **consulted** with him by phone.
- Using my ohm meter, I methodically **tested** all connections, **documented** each step and **diagnosed** the cause to be the distributor, which the mechanic had replaced two months previously and which was still under warranty.
- I **removed** the distributor and returned it, **requesting** that they reinspect the part. It was defective and they gave me another one.
- I **replaced** the distributor, **reset** the timing and turned the key...my car started!
- I systematically and diplomatically **explained** which parts and labor I did and did not need and **negotiated** a refund from my mechanic.

RESULTS = WOW!

1. I received a $700 refund for all unwarranted parts and labor.
2. I solved my problem and once again felt confident I wouldn't be stranded.
3. Now, when I talk to my mechanic, I am taken seriously.
4. I gained a great deal of confidence in my problem-solving skills.

SKILLS (STATED)	TRAITS (IMPLIED)
I can:	**I am:**
—solve problems	—analytical
—diagnose	—systematic
—communicate	—curious
—test	—persistent
—negotiate	—assertive
—consult	—persuasive
—experiment	—mechanical

ADAPTING STORY FOR SKILLS-ALIGNED RESUME

NOTE THAT THIS STORY ILLUSTRATES TWO SKILLS. ALWAYS USE THE STORY FORMAT.

THE SKILL: PROBLEM-SOLVING

(What) I **solved a** major mechanical **problem** with my car
(How) By consulting with knowledgeable people, testing all connections with an ohm meter and diagnosing the cause of the problem.
(Wow!) I replaced the defective distributor myself saving $700.

IT LOOKS LIKE THIS ON YOUR RESUME:

I solved a major mechanical **problem** with my old car by consulting with knowledgeable people, testing all connections with an ohm meter and diagnosing the problem. I replaced the distributor myself saving $700.

THE SKILL: COMMUNICATING

I **communicated** with knowledgeable people regarding a mechanical problem with my car, consulting with experts, explaining which parts and labor I did and did not need to my mechanic, and negotiating a refund on unwarranted parts, saving $700.

Page 162

ADAPTING STORY FOR JOB INTERVIEW

Based on our conversation to this point, it seems to me that you need someone in this position who can **solve problems**. Is that right?

What: Let me tell you about how I relentlessly pursed **solving a** mechanical **problem** with my aging Honda Prelude.

How: I **examined** and **tested** several parts and **diagnosed** a problem with the electrical system and took the car to a mechanic who "fixed" it. After having my car towed four times after it had been "fixed," I **decided** to **experiment** on my own. Using my ohm meter, I methodically **tested** all connections, **documented** each step and **diagnosed** the cause to be in distributor, which the mechanic had replaced and which was still under warranty. I **returned** the distributor and **requested** that they test it. It was defective and they gave me another one. I **installed** the new distributor and my car started!!

results were (say this every time):

I negotiated a $700 refund for all unwarranted parts and labor.
Now, when I talk to my mechanic, I am taken seriously.
I gained a great deal of confidence in my problem-solving skills.

Reality checks (use one or all):

Is this illustration in line with the problem-solving skills you're looking for in this position? I believe this example shows aptitude, interest and skill, all of which you will want in the person you hire. Do you agree?

Adapt the story to illustrate the skill of communicating.

WHY SHOULD I HIRE YOU? ADAPT YOUR STORY TO ILLUSTRATE A TRAIT:

You should hire me because I'm **persistent**. I once had a car that would not start periodically, leaving me stranded. I consulted with knowledgeable people, communicated with mechanics, tested the electrical system and finally replaced the distributor. I didn't quit until I had solved the problem. It seems to me that this is exactly the kind of person who would be an asset to you. Am I right?

ASSESSING SKILLS AND TRAITS: A STORY FROM WORK EXPERIENCE

What I Did: When I was with Actual Telecommunications, I developed a subscriber-loop test system which tests telephone wires that go from the central office to people's homes.

How I Did It:
- I **defined** the system architecture.
- I **selected** and **hired** personnel proficient in both hardware and software applications.
- I **assembled** and managed both the hardware and software development teams while they designed and built the product.
- I **delegated** design tasks.
- I **coordinated** the system integration and tests in our lab before the system was delivered to the customer.
- I **facilitated** the transition to the manufacturer so that more system could be built for future customers.

RESULTS = WOW
1. The system was delivered to the initial customer on time and within budget.
2. After some on-site de-bugging and evaluation, it was ready for customer use.
3. I was very happy with the designs and functionality of the system.
4. Eventually that system provided 85% of the revenue for my division.
5. The system is still in production 15 years later.

SKILLS (STATED)	TRAITS (IMPLIED)
I can:	**I am:**
—define	—detail-oriented
—select	—methodical
—hire	—conscientious
—assemble	—analytical
—manage	—collaborative
—delegate	—industrious
—coordinate	—focused
—facilitate	

Page 164

ADAPTING STORY FOR SKILLS-ALIGNED RESUME

NOTE THAT ONE STORY ILLUSTRATES SEVERAL SKILLS. ALWAYS USE THE STORY FORMAT.

THE SKILL: PROJECT MANAGEMENT
(What) At Actual Telecommunications, I **managed a project** to develop a test system for residential phone wires
(How) by defining system architecture, managing activities of hardware and software design teams and coordinating final system tests.
(Wow!) This product ultimately generated 85% of the division's revenue.

IT LOOKS LIKE THIS ON YOUR RESUME:
At Actual Telecommunications, I **managed a project** to develop a test system for residential phone wires by defining system architecture, managing hardware and software design teams and coordinating final system tests. This product ultimately generated 85% of the division's revenue.

THE SKILL: TEAM BUILDING
At Actual Telecommunications, I **built hardware and software design teams** to develop a test system. Defined skills, selected from applicant pool, interviewed and hired personnel, producing a test system which ultimately generated 85% of the division's revenue and is still in production 15 years later.

THE SKILL: COORDINATING At Actual Telecommunications, I co-ordinated the efforts of software and hardware design teams to develop a test system by delegating tasks and facilitating transition to the customer. The customer was pleased and the product generated revenue for the next 15 years.

ADAPTING STORY FOR JOB INTERVIEW

I've talked with several people in your department about this position and the feedback is that the successful candidate must have solid **project management** skills. Is that a fair assessment?

(What): I'd like to tell you about **managing a big project** at Actual Telecommunications to develop a test system for residential phone wires. **(How):** I first **defined** the system architecture. I then **selected** and **hired** personnel proficient in both hardware and software design.
I **built** software and hardware **design teams** from the personnel pool. I **motivated** my teams, **delegated** design tasks and **monitored** progress. I **coordinated** the system integration and lab tests before delivering the system.

The results were (say this out loud every time):
The system was delivered to the customer on time and within budget. Eventually that system provided 85% of the revenue for my division. They system is still in production today—15 years later. I was proud of the design and functionality of the system.

Reality checks (use one or all):
Does this example illustrate the kind of **project management skills** you're looking for? How does this example relate to your position?

Adapt the story to illustrate the skills of team building and coordinating

WHY SHOULD I HIRE YOU? ADAPT YOUR STORY TO ILLUS-TRATE A TRAIT

You should hire me because I'm very **industrious** and **focused**. At Actual Telecommunications, I built software and hardware design teams to develop a test system for residential phone wires, facilitated team activities, tested the new product in our lab and delivered it to the customer. That system is in production today (15 years later) and provides 85% of revenue for the division. I'm sure you are looking for someone who is that focused on results. Am I right?

Page 166

ASSESSING SKILLS AND TRAITS: A CHILDHOOD STORY

What I Did: I **developed** my paper route into a profitable business.

How I Did It:
- I **reasoned** that homes within my geographic area that were not subscribing to the paper outnumbered my current subscribers by a four- to-one ratio.
- I **analyzed** that I needed to sign up just one-fourth of those homes to make a handsome profit.
- I **developed** a list of those households most likely to subscribe and **targeted** them for promotion of the Long Beach Press Telegram.
- I **determined** how best to **influence** a positive decision to subscribe. If I could offer them a one-week free subscription, they might sign for a trial subscription.
- I **assessed** the best way to obtain enough papers to be able to offer the free subscriptions and **negotiated** with other paperboys and our route supervisor for their extra papers.
- I **provided** the targeted homes with their free papers and enclosed a note introducing myself and the trial subscription.
- I **"porched"** their papers—a service reserved only for those customers who tipped.
- At the end of the trial week, I visited each home and **persuaded** them to try a three-month subscription.

RESULTS = WOW!
1. Within one year subscriptions more than doubled, from 58 to 130, or about 125%.
2. I earned "Paperboy of the Year" award two consecutive years.
3. My monthly income tripled as we were paid on a sliding scale: more homes meant more commission per newspaper.
4. My parents were proud and bragged about me to their friends.
5. I was a popular kid because I always had money in my pocket.

SKILLS (STATED) **I can:**	TRAITS (IMPLIED) **I am:**
—reason	—analytical
—analyze	—determined
—develop	—industrious
—target	—resourceful
—assess	—persuasive
—provide	—bright
—persuade	—competitive
—influence	—disciplined
—negotiate	—results-oriented

ADAPTING STORY FOR SKILLS-ALIGNED RESUME

THE SKILL: BUSINESS DEVELOPMENT
(What) I **developed** my paper route into a profitable business
(How) by targeting homes for trial subscriptions and persuading prospects to try a three-month subscription.
(Wow!) Within one year I increased customers from 58 to 130 and tripled my income.

IT LOOKS LIKE THIS ON YOUR RESUME:
I **developed** my paper route into a profitable **business** by targeting homes for trial subscriptions and persuading prospects to try a three-month subscription. Within one year I increased customers from 58 to 130 and tripled my income.

THE SKILL: SELLING
I **sold** 125% more newspapers in one year by targeting homes on my route for trial subscriptions and persuading prospects to try a three-month subscription. I increased customers from 58 to 130 and tripled my income.

ADAPTING STORY FOR JOB INTERVIEW

I realize that you need some in this position who can **develop new business** for your organization. I've been developing businesses since I was twelve years old!

(What): Let me tell you about the time I turned my paper route into a viable, profitable business.

(How):
- I **analyzed** that homes within my geographic area that were not subscribing to the paper outnumbered my current subscribers by four-to-one.
- I **developed** a list of those households most likely to subscribe to an evening newspaper and **targeted** those homes for promotion of the Long Beach Telegram.
- I **reasoned** that if I offered them a one-week free subscription, they would be influenced to sign up for a trial subscription.
- I **negotiated** with other paperboys and my route supervisor to obtain

Page 169

enough papers for my new one-week subscriptions.
- I **delivered** those papers and enclosed a note introducing myself and the one-week trial subscription and provided outstanding customer service by "porching" their papers.
- I **followed-up** by visiting each home and **persuading** them to try the paper for three months.

The results were (say this out loud every time):
Within one year my subscriptions more than doubled—from 58 to 130 or about 125%! I earned 'Paperboy of the Year' two consecutive years. I was a very popular kid because I always had money in my pocket.

Reality checks (use one or all):
I think this example illustrates my ability to develop business, and shows that I do it quite naturally. Do you agree?

This example, along with those from my adult work life, give you an idea of my business development skills. Are they in line with what you're looking for?

Adapt story to illustrate the skill of selling.

WHY SHOULD I HIRE YOU? ADAPT YOUR STORY TO ILLUS-TRATE A TRAIT
  You should hire me because I've always been **results-oriented** and **industrious**. I had a paper route as a kid and targeted new customers, provided them with trial subscriptions, followed-up with personal calls and doubled my subscriptions from 58 to 130 in a year. I'm sure you want someone in this position who acts upon opportunity and makes money for the company. Am I right?

APPENDIX E

YOUR ULTIMATE INTERVIEW

Review Chapter 1, BEYOND Z

Imagine your interview with the Creator.
What Checkpoints will you talk about?
What specific stories will you tell?
Write your ultimate interview and you will have strong and clear direction to your true North.

persevere.
plan.
strategize.
focus.
breathe.
write.
let go: relax.
forgive.
all this failing...

take a nap.

- mary anne radmacher -

**What would your life be like if you loved your work?
Want to find out?
www.careermakers.com**

For Further Information

On **CareerMakers** Programs and Seminars

Send Inquires to:

careers@careermakers.com
or spiritpress@earthlink.com

To order additional copies of
Want a New, Better, Fantastic Job?

Contact:

8555 SW AppleWay, Suite 130
Portland, Oregon 97225
1-888-244-1055
503-297-6610
careers@careermakers.com

or

1212 NE 26th # 5
Portland, Oregon 97232
503-284-0217
spiritpress@earthlink.net
http://home1.gte.net/artdept/spiritpress.html

What would your life be like if you loved your work?
Want to find out?
www.careermakers.com

This book requires that you do some writing and reflecting. Therefore, we suggest that you use a separate notebook to write exercise outcomes, thoughts and notes. If you think they would be helpful, we are happy to send you pertinent pages such as Target Call sheets, Weekly Action Plan sheets, a Focus Sheet, a laminated copy of Researching and Filtering Questions for your networking notebook, and a poster size Compass for $9.95. (no shipping fee). You may make as many copies of these for your personal use as you wish.

Write, call or email CareerMakers at:

8555 SW AppleWay, Suite 130
Portland, Oregon 97225
1-888-244-1055
503-297-6610
careers@careermakers.com

Your thoughts and notes:

SPIRIT PRESS